# Lance C

# Horizons

First published on ebook Kindle ……..
Copyright © 2013 Lance Clarke

Lance Clarke asserts the moral right to be identified as the author of this work.

The catalogue record for this book is available from the British Library


ISBN: 978-1-291-59619-9

PublishNation, London
www.publishnation.co.uk

**Other books by Lance Clarke**

Thirty Days

Not of Sound Mind

Laka Stvar (Second edition: The Innocents.)

# Acknowledgements

I want to acknowledge five women in my life, beginning with my loving, tender late wife who bravely fought breast cancer which ended our forty-year love affair, my new love who lit a candle that had been all but snuffed out, my mother whose strength and fortitude saw her through the war years and massive changes in society and two beautiful and courageous daughters, each of whom had challenges of their own to deal with.

I am lucky enough to have known many other women, all of whom had to fight through challenging situations and usually hold themselves and a family together. I hope they enjoy these stories, because each of them has a story of their own to tell – far better than anything I could have invented.

*I hope reader enjoy my*

Lance Clarke

~~November 2013~~

*January 2016*

_16 Stories_

# Contents

**Story Titles:**

# TEN

One, two, three…up to ten. Count slowly, don't rush it, keep the discipline. I've always had plenty of that and now I need it more than ever. Just ten and no more, count them and mark the spot, take up the count again tomorrow. Always leaving it to the next day; then count again, mark again and stop. It all adds up.

The number ten is fascinating, part of a centimetre, a perfect number, divisible by two or five, but no other. Napoleon had it right. Metric measures are nice and simple. No complications of twelve, magic numbers or sorcery, ancient Egyptian or Greek symbols; just one to ten and multiples of ten, and the ability to increase that unit infinitesimally.

Now it provides a prop for my survival, a marker; it allows me to pace myself, to keep to a steady focussed routine, indivisible by anyone else but me. Breakfast as usual, exercise in units of ten press ups, ten sit ups, ten of ten different exercises, everything in multiples of ten. I must keep focussed it is the only way to survive. Lunch, then think back to when I was ten years old. Those wonderful days of warmth and brightness – not like the pitch dark – talking with friends, eating watermelons until we wanted to throw up and giggling until our hearts beat fast. No multiples of ten in those heady young days, long before the chaos and seething hatred. Where there was light not dark, fresh air not stale stench, music and laughter not silence. Continue with tens, and after that, go to twenty, then thirty and up to forty. Then back to eleven, twenty one and thirty one and so on. Sequences are important. My age of forty-three gives plenty of reminiscences, I evoke images and events, and then repeat the set three times, adding beautiful details where I can; on the hundredth time I will bring all the memories together as the final discipline.

A new day and another ten, mark the spot by feeling with tender fingers and scratching the cement – it has to be recognisable so I can find it in the dark otherwise all the work was wasted. The discipline has to be strong and one mistake would lead to a loss of the sequence. This would lead to a devastating loss of identity or independence. Think of a star in the blackness of the sky, able to relate its position relative to others in the galaxy. Now think of self. Darkness, no measure of time spent, or to go – just a void. Then the lazy, creeping and seductive need to sleep to blot out the horror of silence. That must be avoided at all costs.

One, two, three and then – deep horror - a lost marker! Keep calm and move fingers backwards and forwards calmly until the last marker is found. Don't panic, keep the heartbeat steady and slow the thoughts to concentrate hard. Then move forward from that last point until the latest is found again.

Joy – it is there.

That overwhelming feeling of success, although it would be a small and insignificant matter in everyday life it assumes monumental importance here. You can't beat me. I am complete. I am whole. I am the centre of this tiny universe, controlling every measurable thing around me including my actions and my very thoughts, stopping at prescribed points and starting again when I dictate a restart.

I started counting to ten when faces were pressed against mine, shouting obscenities, insulting my religion, my family, my sex, my person. I was paralysed with fear and confused. Oblivious to my cries of innocence and with nothing to give them whatever, I had to withdraw or go mad - so I withdrew. Every question on the outside was countered with my new internal discipline; one, two, three and up to ten. Endlessly counting slowly and rhythmically like a mantra until the voices became insignificant and disappeared, as though they were echoes in a tunnel. One, two and up to ten. In those early days the count was repeated over and over again. Block them out, hear nothing, say nothing, nothing to say, just keep on counting.

One, two, three…now I must remain strong by using the sequence of ten. In their frustration they cannot break me, in their determination they devise all manner of indignations, pain and horror to get information I do not have, never had, never will have, would never want. I focus on ten. I discipline ten. I use ten as my guide through the days of hell. I count myself lucky to have made this number my lodestone, its magnetism ephemeral and yet real, it points me in the right direction and I obey this line, even though I set it myself and follow it without question.

All because of numbers. Nine/eleven – iconic shorthand that would excuse a multitude of sins of fools and brush aside rational thought or reason from victims. Let slip the dogs of war – cry havoc, cry pain, cry mercy, cry for vengeance, or cry for humanity. But then crying is useless. Surviving to tell the tale is everything; to tell the world the truth. To tell my story to divide myself by two: my person and my religion. I understand the nine/eleven pain, but my Ten keeps me sane to tell you that causing me pain is not the answer.

Then comes the final ten, of one hundred tens, meaning one thousand bricks in this tiny, fetid, dark cell. Each one of these divisible groups of bricks is full of physical endeavour and coded encyclopaedic memories, the cement to my survival. I wait now. It is almost over. One hundred days solitary confinement, because of a failure to co-operate, where co-operation is impossible. One hundred days of tens to keep me sane and determined to survive.

One, two, three...then the door bursts open and the light pierces my world hurting my eyes and threatening to shatter my brain. Four, five, six...I hear voices, this time temperate, filled with a kind of resigned compassion as I stand before them, straight and defiant. Seven, eight, nine, and my breath falters in my chest and my heart beats wildly. But I walk steadily towards the open door.

Ten!

# Number 18

Margaret walked briskly along Tottenham Court Road in London on her way to her office in Southampton Row, where she worked as an advertising accounts executive. It was a bright morning and the crisp, cold spring air felt raw in her lungs. As she passed large glass fronted store windows, she glanced at her reflection. It showed a woman in a smart navy two-piece suit that hugged a slim figure. The colour made her look more blonde. Confident she looked; confident she was not. The long walk from Paddington main line station seemed a good idea to help ward off mounting low feelings that had dogged her over the last nine months.

For some people, a lack of judgement is a passing irritant that they put right and a vow never to repeat. In Margaret's case it cleaved to her, stubbornly shrouding every decision she made, ensuring the worst result in every instance. If she turned left, the best direction was right, and if she said yes, then the best solution was no.

Margaret's marriage had collapsed, because of an unwise one-night stand and since the separation her finances were very shaky following unwise investments. Her work in advertising paid well, but mortgage payments to buy a townhouse in a smart area in Reading, now worth less than she paid for it, sucked every penny out of her bank account. Now in her late forties, she had lost that zest for life that makes younger people take risks, never regretting the consequences – now she was simply never sure what the risks were. All that was left was the daily grind of work in order to exist.

Selfridges flaunted attractive, elegant and expensive women's items in the large flamboyantly decorated windows and she hurried by – there was no sense in raising her envy rating. Just past the famous store, she glimpsed a scruffy old bag-lady, wearing layers of what appeared to be torn and patched clothing, with more stored in plastic bags gathered around her, squatting in a shop doorway. The grimy old lady looked up at her, cackled and for almost a full minute they stared at each other. To Margaret's disgust she heard the sound

4

of spraying and realised the bag-lady was urinating. She winced, thinking how awful it would be for the shopkeeper to have to clean it up. Quickening her pace past the doorway, she idly wondered what had caused the old lady's demise. The thought of increasing debt made her shudder – any more interest charges and that could be her in a few years time. It didn't bear thinking about.

As Margaret stepped off a curb she let out a yelp. Missing a step she twisted her ankle ever so slightly, but enough to bring a sharp pain that made her limp. She cursed and realised that she would have to take a bus for the remainder of the journey. Just then a number twenty-two bus approached and she half ran and half limped towards a nearby bus stop, waving her hand as she did so. The driver saw her and brought the bus to a halt. After paying for her ticket, she painfully made her way to the only free seat in the middle of the lower deck. As she bent down to rub her ankle her attention was caught by a woman of about her own age arguing with a man who looked very much younger and she overheard pieces of their conversation.

"That's it Michael, I've had it," said the woman, leaning away from the man. "I know what I am doing and I don't want you bleeding me dry all the time. Got it?"

The man looked angry and turned sideways to address her. The woman looked away and was having none of it.

Just as Margaret was beginning to enjoy the duel, which took her mind off her own problems and the pain in her ankle, there was a flash of light and an enormous explosion. The driver's cab seemed to separate from the body of the bus and the upper deck collapsed downwards on the first half of the lower deck. The bus careered sideways and came to a shuddering halt against a letterbox spilling pieces of glass and metal side panels on either side.

At first there was no sound except for the hissing of the steam from the radiator, the whirring of the engine that refused to stop and the sound of glass falling in from the windows or being crunched underfoot as uninjured people stood up. Then she heard screams and awful moans. The scene was terrible. With the separation of the driver's cab, the metal structure collapsed inwards bringing down parts of seats from the upper deck with people on, flattening those who had been sitting towards the front of the lower deck. Blood was everywhere, but mostly from the passengers who had been on the upper deck where the bomb had exploded.

Margaret had been forced back in her seat and her ribs hurt, glass and debris scratched her face, leaving trickles of blood in lines down to her chin. Her ears were ringing so much it hurt. She started to shake and couldn't control herself. Standing up was difficult and the sharp pain from her ankle made her fall in the aisle and as she tried to get up her legs gave way. On her hands and knees, she felt pieces of shattered glass everywhere. Looking up through tear-filled eyes, she spotted a large ladies handbag and she grasped it to enable her to rest on something to protect her fingers as she pushed herself up. Then a pair of hands caught her under the shoulders and pulled her to her feet, half carrying her out of the debris.

"It's all right love, come on now, out of all this, don't let's hang around," said a young policeman who had been passing in a police car and rushed to help. He and his companion were getting the injured out of the bus and well away from the scene to the safety of a store twenty metres away. Margaret was guided into the store and seats were quickly put out for survivors. The street was now full of ambulances and police cars with blue lights flashing. There was also the unmistakable sound of shop alarms that had been set off by the explosion, so many of them all ringing like crazy, making the whole scene quite surreal.

Then she fainted.

It was now three weeks since the explosion and Margaret was just getting back into her stride. She cried at first, but it was a mixture of anger and frustration at her recent bad luck as well as the horrific experience. Terrible as it was, the explosion just seemed to underline the state of her life at present. She cursed the world at large. She cursed her miserable existence. She cursed the mindless bastards who had committed the pointless terrorist atrocity.

There had been thirty casualties. Eighteen dead bodies were found, but only seventeen had carried identification, the eighteenth person was still unidentified as of yesterday. Those who were injured ranged from the horrific loss of limbs to cuts and bruises. Margaret was, thankfully, one of the 'cuts and bruises' groups.

It was Saturday and her latest boyfriend Jim was busy making a curry and watching football at the same time on the kitchen television. He was a nice guy, a bit possessive and very homely, but a genuine sort. Margaret was bored with watching television and decided to sort out some of her belongings. She left Jim to his culinary pursuit and the odd cheer when his team scored a goal - which wasn't that often.

As she ambled into her bedroom, her eyes fell on the clear plastic bag given to her by the police after she left hospital. In it were her gloves, scarf and sundry items like her watch and a bracelet and even her torn tights. But there was also something else that she didn't immediately recognise. As she moved closer she remembered what it was. It was the handbag she picked up immediately after the explosion.

She rummaged to the bottom part of the plastic bag, brought it out and opened it. Inside was the usual assortment of items one would expect in a ladies handbag: make-up, tissues, tampons, a pen and notebook and a mobile telephone. There was also a purse with about a hundred pounds in cash, a credit card in the name of Elayne Chantelle and two photographs taken in a cheap photo booth, showing a smiling brunette aged about forty. She recognised the picture. It was the woman she had seen arguing with the younger man on the bus.

Margaret felt a tingle as she fingered the mobile phone which was blank and out of charge. Did it belong to a dead person? How could she have forgotten this stuff? She should contact the woman, or, in the worst case the family and return the bag. Trying to think of the correct action to take gave her a headache. She got out a mobile phone multi-charge set of plugs, selected the correct unit, connected it and then plugged the mobile phone into her wall socket. The phone blinked into life as the energy fed into its body and after a prompt on the screen, she entered four zeros as the password, which was accepted - another person too lazy to set up a familiar number. She stared at the pulsating bar on the right of the screen as the mobile received the charge.

Jim called up to her. "Curry time, ten minutes and counting."

"Okay, down soon," she shouted.

With a few moments to spare, Margaret decided that it was reasonable to use the mobile to call the woman's home. She quickly flipped through the 'names', but couldn't find any name like Chantelle. The next best thing to do was to move to the message box. Once into the box she read several messages and finally fell on one that said, *"See you at home tonight – sorry I have to work late. Where are you today then? Alex. xxx"*

She reviewed the contacts and the name Alex had two entries, one matched the text message and noted as 'Alex Mob' and another was a landline number under 'Alex Home'. She felt satisfied that she had found a relative and dialled the number. It rang for about a minute and a man answered.

"Alex Robinson."

"Oh, I'm sorry, I expected someone called Chantelle."

The man sounded irritated. "What is it you want? Money? There's no Chantelle here, in fact as of today there's only me. You probably know already, that's why you are calling I presume, that my wife was identified as the eighteenth victim on the London bus explosion. Number bloody eighteen they said. How did you get this number?"

"I, er, it's a mobile, and I...well I wanted to ask...Elayne Chantelle...you see..." Margaret couldn't get the words to form coherently and they fell from her mouth in a jumble.

"Ah, so you are the bastard who nicked her handbag so that she couldn't be identified causing me three weeks of misery. She wasn't supposed to be in London, she was working in Leeds. What were you hoping for, reward money, and newspaper fame perhaps? Whatever you want, you can fuck off, today is the worst day of my life and I don't intend to have it spoiled even more by dealing with scum like you."

The line went dead.

Margaret was confused, upset and shaking. When she heard Jim coming upstairs she hurriedly put the mobile and other contents into the plastic bag, which she then put into the rear of her wardrobe. Jim came into the bedroom.

"My goodness, you look white," he crossed the room and took her in his arms. "I think that it's back to bed for you. We can curry-nosh a little later."

She fell into his arms and sobbed.

It was another week before Margaret could face opening the handbag again. She also gathered together all the newspaper reports about the casualties and the eighteenth victim had been identified as Carys Robinson, not Elayne Chantelle. Margaret checked the photographs in the press and the dead were now all accounted for. She recognised the woman from the photograph in the purse. There was no mistake it was the same person. Was she leading a double life – she had to be? Her companion was identified as a young up and coming hairdresser who worked in the West End of London.

Margaret had her reasons for returning to the purse and it wasn't just curiosity. She wanted some water following a long afternoon nap and as she passed a table in the kitchen, she happened upon copies of bank statements behind the toast rack. They showed her finances were deeper in trouble than she had realised. Her stomach churned at the thought of her endless financial pressures. Then she remembered the credit card in the purse in the name of Elayne Chantelle.

She pulled the credit card and notebook out of the purse and propped them on her writing desk. Then she switched on her computer and typed in 'Elayne Chantelle'. Within minutes, Google threw up several entries, but one caused her eyes to widen; she identified a wealthy widow, worth millions of pounds, mostly inherited from a wealthy shipping family, who had homes all over the world. The millionairess' face seemed familiar and she wracked her brains as to where had she seen it before. Various entries described Ms Chantelle as a secretive and reclusive person, hardly ever seen, who only ever communicated with her representatives by email or telephone. There was a history of severe mental problems and many embarrassing and eccentric incidents that made the newspaper headlines in Paris, New York and Madrid. Many of her friends were quoted as fearing for her safety. She had been discharged from a mental hospital in London about two years ago and nothing had been heard from her since.

Margaret stared at the picture on the internet web page again and again, she was sure that there was something familiar about the facial features. At first she couldn't put her finger on it. Then she yelped. "My God. It's the bag-lady!"

Could it really be the scruffy old lady she had seen squatting in the doorway near Selfridges? The unmistakable aquiline nose and deep set, sad looking eyes and wide mouth in the picture of Elayne Chantelle matched her image of the bag-lady.

Her mind raced. She felt bad and yet knew that there was a possibility of financial gain and it would hurt no one. Desperation drove her on. Opening the notebook, she flicked through the pages. Why would Carys Robinson carry a credit card in the name of Elayne Chantelle and why was she in London when her husband thought she was in Leeds?

It was obvious. She was milking Ms Chantelle's bank account and having a jolly good time with a handsome young lover without her husband knowing.

Well, if this Carys could do it, then so could Margaret. She closed her eyes as if asking for forgiveness, but knew that it had to be done. All this debt had to end and an opportunity now presented itself.

She continued to flick through the notebook and found nothing that would give any clue to a pin number. Where the hell was it? Most people needed a friendly reminder and it was usually a birthday or some other type of reference, but there was nothing. Then, when she reached the back of the book, she noticed some characters in the form of dots and dashes.

.---- ..--- ..... ----.

It was all nonsense to her. She wrote down the characters and returned to the information on the web about Elayne Chantelle. The more she read about her life the more she pitied her. She had suffered an over-bearing bullying father, privileged schooling, plenty of money, four husbands all of whom tried to cheat her, and a considerable drink and drug habit. And now it looked as though she spent her days on the streets of London, living and urinating in doorways.

She was absorbed by the information in front of her when she heard footsteps on the stairs. It was Jim and she hadn't heard him come home. Quickly, she gathered together the items and pushed them into an empty drawer then closed the Internet window on Elayne Chantelle. Jim entered the room and waved a large bunch of white chrysanthemums.

"Here we go Marg's, flowers to cheer up a brave and lovely lady," he said, and with a flourish he bent down and kissed her gently. "Hey, what's this then? I haven't seen Morse code since I was a sea cadet. These are numbers."

Margaret tried not to look impatient.

"Oh, it's just some figures I saw on the internet. What are they?"

"Er, well, it's, let's see, **1 2 5** and, ah yes, **9**. More like a historical year of reference?" Jim said, raising his eyebrows.

"Oh, it's really nothing, just something I found. By the way, I'm feeling much better, so why don't we go out to a pub for a bite tonight. I know money is tight, but, heigh ho, let's have a bit of fun."

Jim smiled broadly. "Well done Marg's the pub it is then, how about the Crab and Dragon?"

Margaret waited for Jim to leave the room, then she made a note of the numbers: 1,2,5 and 9. Her hands closed tightly around the cash from the handbag. She would take him out for a bite to eat, after all, he was a sweet chap and deserved a treat. Besides, she now needed to get back into action.

Margaret came out of her company headquarters on Southampton Row, unfolding her umbrella against the light rain. Their conduct during her convalescence was impeccable and when she asked for two more weeks on full pay, they agreed without demur. Jim thought that she was back at work, but she had things to do. Firstly, she made her way to a large department store that had a number of credit card machines in the foyer. After a short wait, she walked to a vacant machine and nervously inserted the card. Then came the prompt for the pin number and she held her breath before entering **1 2 5 9** and waited.

It was accepted.

Her heart skipped a beat when the cash-point then prompted her for a sum to withdraw and she asked for £200 and an account balance. She waited again. The green light flashed and she took her card, then the cash arrived along with the receipt and account balance.

After putting the cash into her pocket, she clutched the receipt and account balance and moved to a nearby bench. She sat down and glanced at the paper in awe. The account had a balance of £2,359,332. Her heart beat faster as her mind raced through the three thousand-pound overdraft and the mortgage of two hundred and fifty thousand pounds.

Margaret stared at the screen and knew she had a lot of planning to do – a cover story, a fallback position and so on. How stupid she thought herself. She was going to rob someone's account, and yet she was already making plans for her defence should she be caught. Perhaps she could argue post traumatic stress following the explosion? After breathing deeply, she calmed herself and decided to go for a good lunch.

Over the next few weeks Margaret withdrew almost five thousand pounds. Clearing her overdraft was a joyous experience and she programmed her diary to gradually remove funds to pay off her mortgage over the next six months. This left seven months until the end expiry date on the card after which time an address would need to be given for the new card – that might prove difficult and so it was best to plan her withdrawals carefully.

The only sour note remaining in her life was, perhaps not surprisingly, Jim. He had been content to look after her, but when she began to return to normality, the situation changed. Being confident and thrusting is not what some men like in a woman. Jim needed her more than she needed him. He noticed that Margaret was spending a lot of money and resented her newfound wealth. The moods and sulks were too much for Margaret to put up with. She was now almost debt free and as happy as could be; they inevitably argued and she dumped him. It was a messy affair with lots of shouting and emotion and at one time even the neighbours intervened. But she didn't care at all, why should she? Her life was different now. Everything was so much better. Jim tried to make regular contact with her, pleading to talk things over, but she turned him down flat. He became emotional and angry, especially when she lost patience with him and said some pretty awful things. Then he ceased calling her.

It was almost a month later during a pampering session at the Nirvana Spa near Reading that Margaret met Phillipe, a moderately well off Spanish businessman who had relocated to the UK for a few years. He was all she wanted, handsome, athletic and financially independent.

It didn't take long for them to share a bed. His athleticism and experience coupled with her new freedom and abandon, led to sexual moments of Olympian magnitude. Sometimes it was hard to go to work the next morning, but she had to maintain a sense of normality, for the time-being at least. Margaret went to work because she had that awful and yet irrational feeling that things might go wrong and she needed the security of paid work, she couldn't quite let go of the employment lifeline, working class habits die hard and she hadn't quite got the hang of being rich.

All in all, her life was now in some kind of balance and she enjoyed spending, clearing what remained of her debts and dallying with Phillipe - it was all so much fun. One night at dinner, at Simpson's on the Strand, she knew he had something on his mind.

"Margaret," he said steepling his hands and pursing his lips in that funny way he always did when talking about serious things. "I like you very much and, well, some day I need to go back to Spain. We seem to be getting on and I ..."

She froze for a moment. It was beginning to dawn on her that he wanted to marry her and this was not something she wanted. She was just beginning to enjoy the freedom that money gave her and did not want to have to share her space with someone else. Later, perhaps, but not now.

"Phillipe, if you are going to ask me to marry you then you are going to have to wait," she tapped his hand lightly with a bread stick. "I am enjoying my life and being with you, but I don't want to be tied down just yet. So let's wait and see how things develop shall we?"

Phillipe winced. Used to getting his own way, his business arrogance led him to believe that he would win her come what may. He miscalculated and didn't like it.

"As you wish, Margaret, but I must say that I am disappointed, very disappointed."

She tried to thaw the chill between them and paper over the cracks, but failed and the evening ended quietly with no more than a peck on the cheek when they parted.

Margaret went to her car parked nearby, got in and drove away at speed, cheeks burning with indignation. Who the hell did he think he was? Was he the only man who was good in the sack? Was she to be so grateful for this slick Spanish businessman's attention that she should fall at his feet or what? Did he expect her to rush after him? Well, no way buffalo, not her!

Indignation turned to anger and she braked hard, turned around, and drove into an available parking space near Covent Garden. After parking, she walked back to the Strand. It felt good to be independent enough to be able to say, '*Sucks to the world.*' If it was too late or she had tippled a bit too much, she would book into a hotel - the Ritz perhaps, why not?'

Looking up she saw her favourite pub, The Coal Hole, and went in. The warm air hit her face and good memories enveloped her. The laughter and great times she and colleagues enjoyed on Friday evenings when she was much younger, especially when a new contract had been signed, flooded back. It was almost as though their ghostly faces greeted her at every corner of the pub.

Squeezing her way to the bar she ordered a large gin and tonic and looked around. It wasn't long before two young men sidled up to her and made small talk.

"What's a nice young lady like you doing on your own then?" said the taller of the two men. She laughed and said she could be their mum, but felt flattered by their attention and why not, she was still attractive and had a good figure. Buying the drinks made her feel better, and in control – she liked that. The boys responded with humour and the odd accidental touch on her shoulder, back and, once, her bottom. But she could easily handle it and joined in the banter. She playfully wondered which one of the boys she would take to a hotel – both of them perhaps.

It was shortly after eleven, her head was deliciously hazy and she was beginning to feel pretty horny, and now she had to choose between her two young friends. As she tried to focus, she looked towards the door and saw to her surprise and alarm, the broad figure of Jim, pushing his way towards her, his old-fashioned belted grey raincoat, open and flaying left and right as he strode towards her. He stopped two feet away from her and was red in the face.

"So, it's come to this eh?" he shouted. "Knocking off boys half your bloody age as well as a well-heeled Spaniard?"

The boys laughed and the younger one said, "Who's this then love, the old feller?"

"No he is not. If I were to have a feller then this one wouldn't be it!" She shouted above the din of voices and music.

"Jim, I don't know what you are doing here but piss off," she said, then thought for a moment adding, "How did you know about Phillipe? You've been following me, you sick bastard, haven't you?"

"Don't call me a sick bastard, you were happy enough to let me look after you once upon a time," he yelled back.

By now the boys had sidled off to one side and were chuckling. Margaret felt humiliated.

"You stupid, overweight, boring, bastard. How dare you stalk me? How dare you. If I wanted a man like you, so low in intellect and with a climax to his sexual activity like a speeding bullet, I would need my head examining."

The boys laughed out loud and Jim's face reddened with anger at the unnecessarily piercing insult. Maddened with rage, he reached into his coat and brought out a large knife.

Suddenly, a wide space formed around him as people moved away leaving them facing each other. There was a hush.

"Bitch. You bloody bitch. I'll make you sorry for that," he spat the words at her and waved the blade in her face.

Instinctively, Margaret lashed out with her glass and caught him on the side of his face. The shards of glass pierced his cheek and he yelped as red globules of blood flowed down his neck and onto his sweatshirt. She pushed him to one side and ran for the exit, but wasn't fast enough and he managed to catch her as she ran through the door. They both burst through it and into the street and as they fell to the ground Jim lunged at her body with the knife.

Margaret felt the blade enter between her first and second rib on the left side of her body. It hurt so much she couldn't even scream. Her eyes filled with tears and her vision began to blur, as she tasted blood in her mouth. Jim got up slowly with a look of horror on his face and stared at the bloody knife in his hand. He dropped it and put his hands to his head and howled like a dog. As he did so, Margaret lay sprawled on the wet street her arms outstretched in front of her. In her right hand she held a large handbag and as her grip loosened it slid into the gutter.

A scruffy, dirty young woman with blemished skin and the weary eyes of a drug addict sat watching the mayhem outside the Coal Hole public house. Her name was Ella Jones. She left her smelly blanket and small placard that said, **Hungry please spare some change**, and moved towards the blue flashing lights and milling crowd. Her eyes were fixed on the handbag in the gutter. Before anyone saw what she was up to, she grabbed it, turned around and made off towards Covent Garden holding it close to her chest. Then she stopped to catch her breath, because in her poor condition she couldn't exert herself too much - it was too painful.

She opened the bag and soon located valuables including cash and a credit card, with a slip of paper bearing the numbers, **1 2 5 9**. Looking at the name on the card under the light of a street lamp she wondered whether or not the lady who lay in the street, Elayne Chantelle, was okay. But surveying the scene before her, she became convinced that the lady had died at the hands of some demented man with a knife. Content that this was therefore not exactly stealing, she headed back to her squat, where she would divide the cash between her friends and then see if she could access the credit card. Closing her eyes, her body shook as she anticipated her next long overdue fix – soon she would have as much heroin as she wanted, what bliss!

Ella quickly stumbled away with her prize.

In a nearby alley, an old bag-lady raised her skirts to urinate in the doorway. She watched the girl hurry down the street and smiled quietly to herself.

# DERNCASTLE

Low clouds, grey and puffy, raced across the skyline spraying rain down on the East Yorkshire moor as though a giant garden hose was embedded within each of them. Behind, the sky was lighter and promised to treat the land a little better. But for now it was chilly and wet, and raindrops stung when they hit warm skin.

Gemma was irritated by the cold rain trickling down her neck and as she instinctively moved to button up her jacket, but she stopped her hand and let the rain continue to make her feel uncomfortable. Discomfort brought her back to her senses and today, she was low again and needed that stimulus. So she didn't mind the rain at all, letting it hit her head and run down her face and into her jacket.

Jon Danver, her companion for the day, ran towards her. He was a friendly American who had come to the UK and eventually settled in Derncastle three years ago to develop his writing. An easy going man, he deserved better company. His black Labrador Tess trotted behind him oblivious to the inclement weather.

"Gemma, what the hell's the matter now?" he shouted through the rain and wind. "We're walking along a path and everything is just fine, the next thing I know you go all quiet on me and wander off."

Gemma looked back at him and hunched her shoulders.

"Is that it?"

"Is that what? You don't own me Jon. We're mates and recent mates at that. You just don't bloody well own me Jon."

She stared at him, not out of anger but the kind of stare that belies a vacant hopeless personality.

Jon walked up to her slowly. He had been trying to get to know this enigmatic person for some weeks and found her interesting, funny, intelligent and exceptionally fit, like him. She was also good company most of the time, but for some unknown reason would simply flip or go off in a morose mood. He was at a loss as to what to do or say next. Then he just gave up.

"Look Gemma. What are you – some kind of Goddamned hard-ass who is so superior she can't relate to the opposite sex? Well think on lady. I'm tired of chasing you to find out what's wrong and that's for sure. I'm out of here and if you want to meet up again I'll be in the Granby this evening. If not then that's just fine with me. Enjoy your walk, ma'am."

He strode off, flapping his arms and calling for Tess to follow him, which she did reluctantly. Gemma watched him go, the epitome of the English countryman, with his flat cap almost covering his dark wild hair, and wearing a green Barbour jacket and Wellington boots. She liked him a lot. But she just couldn't let go of the past. It was only when the rain hit her face and brought her back to her senses that she felt enormous guilt. Not just about the way she treated Jon, but her mother and her friends who tried to help her to come to terms with the death of her husband of only three years, Jack. Lovely, Jack, who died suddenly and stupidly in a car accident. Bang. Gone. Just like that.

Jon didn't know though. Gemma had come to her aunt in Derncastle to get away from all the cloying and clumsy cosseting she experienced at home in Sussex. It was understandable that her mother wanted to look after her, but she no longer felt in control of her life and feared she would end up in a perpetual state of mourning. Her aunt, Maureen was sworn to secrecy and for all the locals knew she was just another relative staying over for a few months. But the memory of that dark day, almost one year ago when her life effectively ended with the most tragic of news, haunted her.

Gemma watched the Land Rover drive down the trail and onto the main road, splashing her Metro with mud as it passed. She stood still, fed up and unable to move for a long time. After about ten minutes the rain eventually stopped and the air warmed as the clouds tumbled past and the sky brightened with shards of sunlight reaching downwards to the ground like groping fingers.

She straightened and walked slowly towards her car, the sound of sucking steps squelching along the peaty ground. Inside, she put her head on the steering wheel, gripped it tightly with her hands and sobbed.

The Granby public house was empty except for an elderly couple who came almost every night to drink a solitary black beer and keep

18

warm in front of the large fireplace. Jon sat on a high stool at the bar nursing a local ale in his hands. It was a scruffy, but homely kind of pub, within fifty steps of Derncastle harbour. Its interior had seen several generations of farmers, traders and fisherman sit and talk, smoke and drink, reliving their daily lives. If walls could be genetically imprinted, then the Granby was the sum total of the experiences of a whole community over hundreds of years.

Jon found the most attractive feature was the way that the landlord Jim Brunson, and his wife, Gilly, always greeted customers and would be reaching to pour their favourite tipple before they even ordered a drink. In some ways it reminded Jon of his favourite New York bar. He remembered fondly the barman, a black guy call David, from the Bronx who shared his love of jazz and American football, who fell to a bullet from a drug crazed youth trying to steal cash from the till. That had been the turning point for him and he decamped to the UK, away from gun crime and drugs and, as he described it, stir-crazy American politics. He hadn't regretted it. But English women confused him, especially Gemma.

He put his head back and swallowed the last of a pint of best bitter and Jim brought him another without asking. He had cultivated a taste for British ale and wouldn't touch a Budweiser now for love nor money. As Jon idly tapped his fingers on the bar, the door opened and he saw Gemma come in. He felt a surge of relief and yet did not have a clue what he would say to her. She half smiled at him and headed for a bench seat to the right of the open, blazing fireplace and slightly away from the centre of the pub. Jon turned to speak to Jim and to his surprise he saw him already pouring Gemma's Chardonnay. He smiled and thought, "Heck what a place."

The log fire warmed him as he approached Gemma and he sat next to, rather than across from her.

"Hi. How are you?" she said softly.

"Oh," he said, looking steadily at her. "I'm just fine, except for being totally ignored today by someone who had agreed to go for an uplifting walk in the English countryside. And since I'm a good old American boy, I can tell you, ma'am, I don't like being patronised or ignored by anyone, let alone the opposite sex."

Gemma looked down at her hands. She apologised and touched his arm. Touch always does the trick – with everyone. Then she explained that it was not his fault and he just needed to be patient with her. He didn't understand at first but it was obvious that he was willing to let it drop and give her another chance. They agreed to park all issues now and to have a pleasant evening and they could talk it all over some other time. Some other time, being a pleasant phrase for 'let's just leave it alone.'

As the evening wore on, they both relaxed and enjoyed the ambiance of the Granby. Suddenly, the door was noisily opened and Stanley, the town drunk, stumbled into the pub. He looked crazy, with wild grey hair trying to escape from under his flat cap, and a ruddy complexion, with wild wide eyes.

"Ah! It's the village Yank. How is thee sir?" he said smiling broadly, revealing several gaps in his teeth.

Jon smiled at the thought that he was the village Yank and quite liked the idea. He touched Stanley's outstretched hand and wondered whether he would ever use his hand to eat with ever again.

"Jim, give this man a beer will you," he smiled at Stanley and added, "but I'm having a quiet time so be a good guy and sit somewhere else, huh?"

Stanley readily agreed, happy to claim his first free pint of the night and moved to the opposite side of the pub.

Gemma watched the interaction and smiled. She turned and caught sight of an old couple sitting near the fire. They held hands and spoke occasionally, but often just looked at each other. As she watched them she felt a choke in her throat. That should have been her and Jack in years to come. Knowing, sharing, being together, but not now. She couldn't stop looking at them and slowly their image disappeared in a flow of salty tears.

Jon watched her and was confused.

"Gemma, what the hell's wrong?"

Gemma put her hands to her mouth and tried to breathe more easily.

"Jon, I have to tell you something," she blurted, "and I'm so sorry I held out on you. Seeing that lovely couple sitting by the fire made me feel so very sad. I was married to a man called Jack, and he was killed in an industrial accident a year ago. I just can't get over it. I just can't and ... I need help."

Then she broke down and sobbed. Jon reached out and took her head and put it into his shoulder. He was a tall, but not a bulky man, and his build was such that he was able to almost wrap her in his arms as she sobbed. He said nothing. It would have been stupid. It was best to just let her cry.

After about ten minutes she eased up and he said softly, "Gemma, come with me now. Trust me."

They put their coats on and left the pub. Jon put his arm around her shoulder and guided her towards his flat, a short distance from the harbour. As he unlocked the door, he felt her slightly resist his guidance and he looked at her. "It's okay, I promise."

She relented and they went inside. Thankfully the heating was on and it felt warm and comfortable. He put the lights on and took her coat, before leading her to the couch, gently pressing her to sit down. He went to the sideboard and returned armed with two glasses of scotch then sat down across from her. She regarded him with understandable feminine suspicion.

"Listen to me carefully, Gemma. I am really upset that we have enjoyed a friendship for some weeks now and you didn't confide in me. I don't want to pry, certainly not. But for weeks I thought you were sometimes just plain rude. Now I know why. For the record, I hung around because I really like you. Actually, I really fancy you, isn't that good British-speak for something a little raunchier. See, I'm learning."

Gemma smiled at the easy way that he talked. He always made things sound so easy going and made her laugh, although she knew that was a quality to beware of in a man. She made to speak but he raised his hand.

"Let me finish. I think you should stay here for a while, I really do. I have a spare room and you can have the run of the place. I know your aunt will be upset, but I think that I am the man to help you back on your feet. Will you give me that chance?"

Gemma smiled again and huffed. She raised her shoulders and said, "Jon, you're a lovely man but..."

Jon broke in quickly. "Well that's it settled then. Great! Now listen to me carefully," he reached out and took her hand. "I promise Gemma, I will not try and seduce you. Okay? I want to, I really do - you betcha. But I promise on my word of honour, I will not misbehave – unless you ask me to."

Gemma sat back in the couch and laughed. A Brit couldn't have said that, only Jon – and she trusted him. So she telephoned her aunt who, quite unusually, understood and said she knew Jon and was happy with that. They would make the necessary arrangements tomorrow.

Over the next few hours she and Jon talked more than they had ever done. He dragged out of her every single thing that she liked and disliked and she responded by getting him to reciprocate. And what a surprise it was: he too had many unhappy memories and she found herself helping to exorcise one or two, then, as she was doing so she cocked an eyebrow and paused, wondering whether or not he had led her into this friendly reciprocal counselling. But it didn't really matter, she felt good having at last dispelled the 'grief' demon and now felt able to relate to someone. It was cathartic and she was grateful for it.

Over the coming weeks, Gemma settled into a shared relationship in Jon's harbour flat, occasionally returning to her aunt to talk about what she had been getting up to. Most of all, she and Jon enjoyed walking and they had taken to ambling across the moorland above the village. It was on one of these walks, in the unusually interminable rain so plentiful this year, walking down what was popularly known as the Cut, that Jon noticed something.

"Gemma, have you noticed that the Cut through the wood and down the hill to the village is littered with sticks and logs placed horizontally across the path?"

Gemma looked down the gentle slope that wound its way down to Derncastle and the harbour. Jon was right. Every so often, there was a pack of branches or logs placed horizontally across the path. Sometimes heavy rocks were also laid in the middle of the path.

"Yeah, that's quite strange. I was walking down here the other day and noticed that there were some branches in the way, but not this many."

Together they moved what debris they could as they made their way down towards the village. When they reached to the bottom of the Cut they met Jeffrey and Madeleine Richards the two people responsible for organising the village event that was known as the Wap. A parade of Morris dancers, Mummers, young children and villagers all dressed up in Victorian costume, and young girls in white dresses with flowers in their hair would wind down from a point on the moor along the Cut and into the village before moving to the harbour. The whole event was cobbled together based on several smaller local legends and events that had been long since consigned to history. Jon found all these traditions really 'cute', but nevertheless treated them with respect. He recalled saying something unwise last year to a Morris dancer who then challenged him to drink as much beer as him and complete just a few of the energetic dance routines. Jon drank only three pints of best bitter and did a couple of dances before calling it a day - he limped for a week.

"Hello, each," said Madeleine, brushing her wet hair out of her face. "Dreadful weather, I do hope it stops soon and doesn't spoil the village celebrations at the weekend."

Her husband Jeffrey nodded in support. "Yes, and if I catch the blighter who has been putting this stuff in the way, I'll brain him," and he waved a fist. Madeleine looked up at him and smiled at his sense of community responsibility.

They joked for a while then separated, as Jon and Gemma made their way back to the harbour.

Later that evening, they sat in the Granby sipping some local cider, much to Jon's distaste, having been persuaded to do so by Jim the publican.

"It's a new brew and I want to test it out on customers," he said cheerily.

Gemma leaned across to Jon.

"The village Wap and parade down the Cut is very important to the Richards, I know they put a lot of work into it. I do hope nothing goes wrong."

Jon looked across at the window next to their table and, peering into the darkness, he curled his lip.

"Yeah, me too. But I am afraid it still looks kinda wet I'm afraid. Perhaps it'll pass."

For the next half an hour they talked about the upcoming day's events and whether or not they would dress up. Gemma tried to persuade Jon to wear a big top hat and a black suit on the day of the parade and laughed at his reluctance to do so, saying he would wear a cowboy hat so why not a top hat?

Just then the door to the pub burst open and two teenagers almost fell into the bar. They looked white with fear and the girl was crying.

Jim came from behind the bar and moved them towards the fire.

"What the hell's wrong, kids?" he said motioning them to sit down, waving to his wife Gilly to bring something to drink. She came across with some ginger beer. Jon and Gemma came over and sat with them.

"It was so weird," said the boy, who they knew as Lennie. "We were, like, kissin' and cuddlin' by the giant oak tree in the woods, and saw this kind of strange white light. Then the next thing we saw was a shape moving around puttin' sticks and logs into the Cut. When we stood up, it brushed against us and we screamed and," he gulped cider that had been put in front of him. "I don't mind admitting, we just ran and ran, all the way here."

After comforting the teenagers, Jon and Gemma decided to go and see what all the fuss was about. Several of the villagers urged caution but Jon waved them aside. Armed with torches and dressed in waterproofs they headed off towards the local woods and the Cut. When they got there the rain had stopped and they moved along the sodden path and into the dark trees. As they entered, large drops of water dripped down around them with loud splattering sounds. Jon flashed the torch left and right and made suitable loud manly comments to show that he wasn't in the least bit worried. Gemma tried to do the same, but was beginning to lose courage.

As they reached the middle of the Cut Jon put his hand out to one side.

"There's something there!" he whispered. "Quiet."

He put the torch off then counted to ten very slowly. Then he put it on again. Just as he did so they caught sight of a figure caught in the beam.

"Good grief," shouted Gemma. "It's Stanley. Stanley, come here you fool, what have you been up to?"

Stanley stood there, holding his hand up to his eyes, trying to look into the light. He looked scared too.

Slowly they walked back to the pub and he was shown inside and told to sit down. He too was given something to drink.

"Well now, you silly sod," said Jim. "Tell us what you were doing?"

Stanley quaffed the cider as though it was water, grimaced ungratefully and spluttered. He wiped his lips on the dirty sleeve of his jacket.

"It's 'er. She telled me to do it. I swear. I sometimes sleeps in the woods see. Well I doesn't always get on with sleeping in a tin box that's what I calls my caravan. I got this dry lean-to, see, and the air is fresh. Anyways, this vision comes to me and says that I 'ave to put obstacles in the Cut. She makes me do it. I tried to ignore 'er but she kept comin' back, again and again."

By now he was getting very agitated.

"It started about two weeks ago. I can't get 'er out of my mind. I must be goin' mad."

He stopped jabbering and reached for a refilled glass of cider in front of him taking more noisy gulps.

Gemma was intrigued, but Jon was sceptical and winked at her mouthing "...he's pissed..."

She reached out and touched Stanley's hand and his gaze became less frantic as he looked at her.

"Stanley, what did this lady actually say and what did she look like?"

He took another gulp of cider.

"She said I had to block the Cut, save the children, stop the deluge, and some other stuff that I couldn't understand. Her's called Catherine, that's it, Catherine Bolan, 'er said so. But I doesn't like ghosts, no not me. My mother was a clairvoyant and spiritualist and she always respected the spirits. That's why I was so afraid – still is mark you."

He quaffed the remainder of the cider and held the glass up hopefully. Jim smiled and waved a hand. "Two on the house is quite enough Stanley, I'm not a bloody charity."

Stanley shrugged his shoulders and looked around for another mug to buy him a drink. Gemma duly obliged and Jon and Jim winced with disapproval.

"Stanley, what did she look like? Forget all the other stuff," said Gemma ignoring everyone else and concentrating on him.

"She was, well, kindly faced with a long nose. Long fair hair braided and platted and she wore a large light coloured shawl over her head and the top of her body. I didn't see 'er blouse of nothing, but she was wearing a long black or dark skirt. She sort of glowed and that's how I knows for sure that she ain't 'uman and 'twe'rn't a joke by someone. I was and still is mighty scared."

Stanley was escorted back to his caravan and told not to sleep outside in bad weather again. He was also reminded about the evils of too much drink and most of those who remained in the pub that night put the whole incident down to a surfeit of cider, beer or anything alcoholic.

Naturally discussion went on well beyond closing time with some people talking up ghostly apparitions of the past, whilst others were more pragmatic and treated it as a joke. They had a laugh at Stanley's expense.

The next day Gemma let Jon make breakfast before he had to go to a meeting with his publisher who had decided to make it all the way down to Derncastle to discuss his new novel. They both left together and she decided to walk about the harbour. It was about half an hour later that she came across a small curiosity shop, full of bric-a-brac, but not quite the things that most tourists would be looking for. The window was full of old books, clothing, some small ancient furniture, porcelain and countless photographs of different sizes. It was the photographs that intrigued her.

As she went into the shop a small bell tinkled. She smiled to herself. That had to be the right noise for this shop, not the disembodied musical chimes or buzz of the novelty shops in the village – but a simple bell. After a few minutes an elderly lady came into the rear of the shop. She was quite old and very bent over. Despite the warmth of the day, it was rainy, again, but very mild, she wore a heavy blue cardigan.

"Can I help you my dear?" she said in a slightly creaky voice. As she looked up and through her spectacles, Gemma noticed her sparkling blue-grey eyes.

"Thank you. I was passing and I wondered it you had any old pictures of the Cut from years back?"

The old lady smiled back at her. "Well, I have one or two. Mainly from the time when I was a child and we used to use it as a walk in the summer and a toboggan run in the winter. We used to have lots of snow in those days of course."

She turned and after looking around the small shop found what she was looking for, it was a small brown suitcase. After rummaging inside she said triumphantly, "Ah! Here we are." Smiling broadly she held up a handful of photographs. "Have a look at these."

Gemma took the photographs proffered her and flicked through them. The Cut was indeed an important part of the village. The photographs showed children running, chasing and sledding down the slippery slope. But there was nothing of the local village parade or festivities currently being planned. She asked the old lady about it.

The lady smiled and raised her nose as people do when they know something of interest.

"Well now, my dear. That's because, the village committee in their wisdom, dredged up various historical celebrations and put them together to make one new village event. They call it the Wap. I must say I was a little against it at first, but it does seem to be a lot of fun and is very popular. It started about five years ago."

Gemma understood. The old lady pushed the small battered suitcase towards her and let her rummage through the old pictures. It was enthralling. There was so much history in the photographs, all captured in sepia or black and white. Scanning each photograph, she felt as though she was beginning to know and belong more to Derncastle. After looking at a dozen or so, she stared at one photograph in particular. It was of some kind of market stall outside the village library. She knew where that was, but alongside it was another building where the present community centre was now situated. The name engraved into the stone lintel above the door was Catherine House.

The old lady let her keep the picture but could only remember that the building had been demolished in the fifties. She recollected that it was a building named after a woman who had been famous in the village for over two centuries.

When she caught up with Jon and his publisher for lunch they smiled patronisingly when she showed them the photograph and explained how she thought it necessary to pursue the history of the lady called Catherine. They were too deep into the depths of Jon's current novel to listen carefully and she left them after about twenty-five minutes. She went to the library to see what she could dig out of the reference section. It didn't take her long to find a grubby and well-thumbed book entitled, Derncastle Through the Ages.

Excited, she leafed through the pages quickly, looking for reference to a woman called Catherine Bolan - and she found it.

It was a short note alongside a photograph of a woman dressed in a shawl, bearing an uncanny resemblance to the woman Stanley had described the night before. The story was simple and brought into stark relief the history of the Cut. In 1798, this part of the country endured a large amount of rain, more than it had ever experienced before. A village parade of children was destined to take place, through a long thin path through the woods and down into the harbour area, after which flowers would be thrown into the sea. Apparently, there had been an enormous flash flood and water gushed down from the moor above Derncastle in the most enormous deluge. Catherine Bolan was a local shepherdess and for some reason had seen it coming. She ran to the children who were then walking down the woodland pathway and warned them to move onto higher ground in the woods. Sadly, her warning was only partly heeded because some parents felt themselves better educated than a shepherdess to know how to look after their children. They regretted it afterwards and several young girls were swept to their death. Catherine saved two children all on her own, but died of pneumonia some months afterwards. She was remembered by having a building named after her in her honour. The Cut replaced the thin path through the woods after the deluge, remaining an enormous deep scar scoured out of the ground, starting from somewhere on the moor above Derncastle. Gradually over the years, when similar deluges didn't materialise, bits of stone and rubble were removed and it provided a wide and safe passage for people and animals down from the moor. All trace of the past horror was lost and it became an accepted piece of the Derncastle countryside.

Sadly, when Catherine House was pulled down to make way for the community centre just after the Second World War, all public reference to Catherine the Shepherdess was lost. Gemma knew this was the answer she had been looking for and quickly got permission to photocopy the page with the information on it and then rushed back to the flat. Jon was there.

"Jon, just look at all this," she said urgently. "I know you were doubtful earlier and had things on your mind, what do you make of it?"

Jon was patient, and fought back the effect of a good lunch and a bottle of Shiraz, making a pot of strong coffee to help him concentrate. Despite his earlier scepticism and an over-riding thought that Stanley might have read the article in the library and used it to his benefit, he kept an open mind.

Gemma was by now quite excited. "Look Jon. This woman, the Catherine that Stanley saw - and don't forget his mother was a clairvoyant and spiritualist - saved a large number of children. The climate at the time was rainy. It's rainy now. And, more worrying, the village has resurrected various local traditions, and one of them is to use to the Cut to parade down to the harbour."

They both sat in silence. He needed to think carefully about what Gemma was saying.

"And you think that Catherine came back to somehow prevent people from using the Cut because, well, because it could happen again," he looked at his watch, "tomorrow?"

Gemma looked straight at him. "I guess so. It all adds up doesn't it?"

Jon thought for a moment before answering.

"Maybe, honey-bunch, but you try telling the village elders, including the formidable Richards' family, to cancel their arrangements. For a Yank to do that I would risk being tarred and feathered."

Gemma ran her hands through her hair. It did sound so implausible when the case was made in the cold light of day. Yet something was driving her to take action. She stood up and went to the desk they both used and grabbed her road atlas leafing through the pages until she got to one that gave an overview of the roads and countryside around Derncastle. She opened it then yelped.

"Look Jon," she pointed to where Derncastle was situated on the map. "See here, the river Dern winds to the sea from three miles away, but all this area above the village is moorland and obviously the river's source is around there somewhere. But if the source gets too full too quickly, maybe, just maybe, it would find an alternative route to the sea?"

She swept her finger down the map and stabbed it against where Derncastle was situated.

Jon's mouth opened but he didn't say anything. He was now convinced enough to know that it was worth trying to persuade the village people that the parade should be re-routed, but that would certainly not be easy.

Without delaying any further, they made their way to the village hall, where the Wap organisation committee was meeting to put the final touches to the events. As expected, their comments met with cries of derision and anger. The Richards refused to speak to them further on the subject, and most of the shop owners were angry. The parade would go ahead. The girl from out of town and the local Yank had it all wrong. The Cut had been cleared now and the participants were determined that they were gong to continue with the procession despite the weather.

The rain continued falling, heavier now.

Back at the flat Gemma was too stressed to eat. Jon on the other hand ate a plate of bacon and eggs, but maintained his concern, as only men can do. He kept muttering that people who lived with tornadoes, whirlwinds and hurricanes in the Americas never, ever, said that weather could be beaten and yet always went back to their homesteads and built another house of flimsy wood.

"Jon, I think we need to split our efforts in two. If we cannot stop people from marching down the Cut then at least we can maintain some kind of watch on the situation and be ready to warn people. What do you think?"

Jon thought for a moment then put his hands together. He was looking for the best solution.

"Sure. I know what. I'll go to the top of the village and find my way to where we think the water is gathering. If I see anything that needs a warning then I'll give you a call on your mobile, okay?"

"Yes, that will make me feel so much better. I'll walk down with those in the parade and if you call with an emergency then I will get them out of the way. It's all we can do."

Gemma held her hands together tightly and added, "Jon, you do share the sense of danger that I feel don't you?"

Jon took her hand in his. "Gemma, listen to me carefully. I don't believe in spirits or ghosts, okay? But there is something about all this that seems to fit like a well-crafted jigsaw and I don't want to be the one who got it wrong. That's the poker player in me. But perhaps the most important thing to me is that someone I think rather a lot of is worried sick and needs me to take her seriously. It's all about respect. That's where I stand, okay?"

Gemma smiled her gratitude.

That night they didn't go to bed, preferring to lie on the couch in each other's arms, hoping upon hope that the coming day would prove them wrong, and for everything to work out all right.

The day started with bright skies and few clouds. This brought out the children, their mums and dads and of course the traders. Gemma and Jon moved through the gathering crowds and one or two of the organisers threw ribald and sarcastic remarks, like, "That's the Spirit," but they took it on the chin. When they got to the car park, Jon kissed Gemma and made his way to his Land Rover. As he drove off, he turned and blew her a kiss and she touched her lips in return. Then he was gone. Turning slowly she walked towards a group of children making their way to the Cut, dressed in loose fitting white dresses with flowers in their hair. As she smiled and talked to them the sky darkened and, ominously, the rain started falling again.

Jon drove quickly up onto the moor and parked his Land Rover a couple of miles above the village. He had lived in Derncastle long enough to know the lie of the land and walked along a path that he knew intersected the Cut. As he reached that point he became aware that his feet were sinking into the ground. Not mud, but soft spongy ground, each step squeezing large amounts of water over his Wellington boots and sucking them into the peat. After a while his feet became so bogged down he found it difficult to walk. He instinctively knew what was happening. Looking through the falling rain to his left he was shocked to see the ground shimmering in the daylight, it was almost like a vast water meadow, but he was concerned. Water meadows don't usually form this high up or on the edge of a slope for that matter.

When he got closer to the intersection of the Cut he saw that there had been a fall of mud and rock blocking it completely. So that was it. What appeared in front of him now was a naturally formed dam, with a small lake behind it holding back a giant sponge full of water. He scrambled through the brambles and boggy ground and as he reached the Cut, he saw to his horror that water was beginning to flow over the top of the debris. By now he was soaking wet and covered in mud and all of a sudden his feet lost their grip and he slid down the sides of the channel on his back. He got up unsteadily, trying to keep his balance in the slippery mud and reached for his mobile phone, his sticky fingers trying to dial Gemma's number.

She answered and he started to speak. "Gemma, listen you were right. There's a veritable lake up here and ..."

Before he could say more she heard him swear and yell out in surprise. She shouted down the phone but it went dead. By now she was halfway up the Cut and looked down at her feet in horror. A slow trickle of water had formed a smooth flow. The children thought it funny and were jumping up and down in it. The Mummers cursed it and were removing the bells from their shoes. There was nothing for it. She yelled hard.

"Get out of the Cut now, quickly. I just had a call from the police and they say it's an emergency. It's a flood. Get out now."

At first no one listened. Then more sensible parents began to move their children up the steep sides of the path and to higher ground. To Gemma's relief a man came running through the woods screaming much the same thing. He had been walking his dog and had seen something happening.

Then the world seemed to erupt. There was a rumbling and water sluiced down the path nearly knocking over the adults who were already scrambling out of the way having pushed children to safety. As Gemma turned she saw a little girl stranded as her mother tried to save two of her own but without hands to save the third. As Gemma reached the child, the water swept them both of their feet and they slid down the Cut. Holding the child tight to her chest she cushioned her from bumping into the sides of the path and was about to get up as they reached level ground, when a large plume of water swept her off her feet. By the time she reached the bottom of the hill an enormous pool had formed and she was able to swim to one side and gain enough purchase to haul herself and the child out.

By now a horrified crowd had formed and some women screamed. She shouted at them.

"Get out of the path of the water, this pool will fill and it won't hold back the flow. Go on get out of the way. Now!"

She was aware she was screaming. But the people around her understood and scattered in all directions, shouting alarm to others further back.

Gemma held the child tightly to her and tried to stop her crying. What had happened to Jon?

All of a sudden there was a loud crash. A tree had been uprooted and tore down the cut like a missile, pushed by an even greater force of water behind it. It entered the newly formed pool at the base of the Cut but catapulted high in the air, one of its branches demolishing half a red telephone box as though it was made of balsa wood. Then it lodged between the corner of a house and a stone wall. The gush of water increased in intensity and debris of large stones, trees and mud, crashed down and through the narrow passageway leading down through the town to the harbour. Gemma handed the little girl to a woman who was making her way up the stone stairs of her boarding house. But she couldn't follow her. She had to look for Jon.

After only two minutes the flow had increased to a torrent and the full force was moving everything in its path, including cars and even an empty skip. These in turn crashed into shop fronts and road-signs like ancient battering rams, reducing anything in their path to rubble. Gemma stared up at the Cut. Then, through the falling rain she saw Jon's red lumberjack shirt. He was clutching a large log, hanging on to one side for all he was worth. Her heart was in her mouth as she realised that he would need to get away from the log that was presently saving him, to avoid being crushed inside the debris-crowded passageway where the water was now flowing to the streets on the way to the harbour.

"Not another loss, no God, not another loss," she thought. Then, quite suddenly the log caught on the side of the half demolished telephone box barely twenty yards from her and she screamed Jon's name so hard she nearly burst her voice box. He looked up and saw her. She waved frantically for him to let go of the log and hold onto the remaining metal side of the telephone box, pointing to the vortex of debris-laden water funnelling into the passageway. He looked weak and her heart skipped a beat, but he managed to pull himself against the now slowing current towards the side of the telephone box – then he let go of the log. Just as he did so it broke loose and careered down the channel, like a bob-sleigh on an icy track. It crashed into the side of the passageway demolishing the wall, revealing the inside of a now flooded house, throwing chairs and furniture around and knocking ornaments and pictures off the walls.

But it wasn't over. Jon was plainly exhausted and his grip was failing. The main force of water was now past but the flow was still fierce and enough to drown a tired man. Gemma looked around her and saw that the shop that sold boating equipment was on the same high street level as her. She ran in and screamed for a life jacket. The owner was all too aware of what was going on and quickly got her one, helping her into it as she explained what she was going to do. He understood what was going on and gathered up a small yacht anchor and attached a long length of rope to it, and both went outside.

"Over there, look, throw the anchor across the water to that large tree, the one that is half submerged. It's bound to get caught up in the branches. Then you tie off the other end of the rope on the lamp post over there," she pointed to the post.

"I'm going to position myself right in front of that man in a red lumberjack shirt. If he let's go I can give him something to grab on to."

The shopkeeper did as he was directed but couldn't help praying that such a stupid idea wouldn't have to be put into action.

Soon, Gemma was pulling herself along the rope and through the fast flowing water, until she reached the middle of the flow and was directly below Jon's now tired and bedraggled figure. He didn't even look up.

Jon hung on for about five minutes, all the time the flow of water buffeted his tired body. By now a crowd had gathered and people were shouting support to Gemma. Then the crowd screamed as Jon's grip loosened and he was pulled away and into the centre of the channel. Gemma braced herself for the blow, but it was bigger than she expected and he hit her with some force winding her so much she gulped a huge amount of water. Her fingers felt as though they were on fire as she struggled to hold on to the rope that cut into her hands.

But Jon's weight was too much for her and her sore fingers were ripped from the rope. At first they both submerged and as they did so, all she could think of was that she was not going to lose another good man and held him tightly to her. Then the life jacket did its job and they both bobbed up to the surface. As they did so they were dashed against the side of the passageway and she felt her head crack against the stone. Still she held on to Jon, her head buzzing like crazy and her body aching.

All the time she kept repeating through gritted teeth, "I'll never give up, I'll never give up." Thankfully, there was no more debris in the descending water to act like loose torpedoes and their bodies bobbed up and down on the surface, prevented from being sucked under by the sturdy life jacket. Then after a while the flow widened out as it made its way down to the harbour. By now several men had formed a chain to ferry people out of harm's way and they saw Gemma and Jon coming towards them. They gathered them up easily, hauling them to safety. The last thing she remembered before she blacked out was a kindly young man wrapping her in a blanket, saying, "You're a bloody heroine. Are you all right love?"

The cotton sheets felt cool and comforting as Gemma opened her eyes slowly and she stretched, ready to enjoy another day of recuperation in Jon's flat, attended to by the occasional visit from the district nurse. The pain in her head had subsided and apart from cuts on her hands there was no lasting damage. The rest of her body was unbroken, but badly bruised. Jon had been very lucky. At the top of the Cut when the dam had broken he had been swept off his feet and nearly made it to safety several times only to be dragged back by the force of the onrushing water. But it had exhausted him. He would have drowned had it not been for Gemma. She saved him. She did something for somebody else in need – she had broken that ring of dependency and vulnerability. She was whole again.

As she gazed out of the window she heard a sound as Jon peeped into the room.

"My, oh my. I thought you would be asleep again. Instead, you look, well, you look just fine. Bright and sparking in fact."

Gemma smiled broadly and stretched. "Yes, I feel it. I really do. I'm just being lazy and, well, kind of thoughtful."

She half sprawled across the bed holding the sheet to her chest allowing her legs to remain uncovered up to her thighs. Jon's eyes roamed. He noticed the chair under the window onto which her nightie had been thrown.

"There's just one problem," she said, with a twinkle in her eye.

"And that is?" he said inquisitively.

She pouted and put on a fake American southern drawl.

"Well, sir, I do declare. I 'member some time back this beau sayin' to me, all sassy like, that he would not misbehave – unless I asked him to. You know sumthin?" she paused for a moment and cheekily added, " I'm askin'."

Jon slowly closed the door.

# TRADING

It's different now. I can do it and do it well. Now I have what the others want. Most of them crowd around me, faces eager to gain my attention and to enter into a trade. They wave their commodities at me to get my interest.

Three for two, or even three for one if their goods are less valuable. I must think on my feet. It is about values, numbers and my ability to deal with stock. It excites me. It pleases me.

I know everything about my commodities, description, availability of stock or shortage of it, so increasing value. Sometimes I give away items to attract business, sometimes I bargain hard - I walk away if necessary. Then they come running, crowding me again, hands reaching out with cards, voices loud and persuasive. But I silence them in negotiation. One of them clings to me reassuringly, because he is younger and more vulnerable; I think he wants my protection and to learn from me. That feels good.

There is little time before the bell ends the session, an intrusion into my world, but one that I see that is necessary – there should be a break from trading. Besides, it gives me time to think of my next move and it must not get in the way of my other responsibilities – and I can wait.

A face is close to mine. He resents yesterday's trade and wants to change. I cannot do that yet. He is upset and his face contorts between anger and tears. He seems desperate. I can deal with that comfortably now. I just smile at him. But it was not always that way.

When I knew nothing about the commodities I was outside the groups that prowled the trading area. They seemed so strong in knowledge, that it seemed to pump their veins with confidence and they strutted, held heads high, scoffing at those less aware. I felt like an outsider and weak. I hated it.

Now I am strong. Not of arm, but of mind. Now I am relaxed and can deal with the others with confidence - self-assured because my route to success is to know more than they do and to use that knowledge effectively. It is different now. They seek me out. They rush around sometimes, swinging their bags or shouting to each other as if to distract me from my dealings. Some ask me questions and I answer, quietly and precisely, and they look at me in awe. I know my stuff

Time is short now. I can see that they know it too and rush to gain the last deal before the bell goes sorting cards, reaching into pockets. I trade quickly in the last few minutes – that is the best time to trade – when they are in a hurry. The detractor returns, this time contrite and appealing. I have traded successfully already and made good deals, so I give him what he wants and so we break even. He thinks he has won and tells his friends. I don't mind. Tomorrow he will be back and I will get the card I want from him with ease. A golden dragon claw.

Finally, she appears, and rings a hand-held bell. A human siren who only knows what time it is and that we must enter the building. I know differently. I know the bell signifies the end of trading. A pause in the important process of effectively communicating and dealing with my fellows; I need to take that into adulthood.

But for now, I am nine years old and must put away my dolls to face more years of learning - I embrace it. I know the key to success.

*I must trade.*

# SHE-WOLF

Hermione lay in her bed half-asleep, in that dreadful no man's land where it is impossible to descend into any kind of deep satisfying slumber, but equally difficult to rouse oneself to controlled consciousness. It was not surprising that sleep did not come easily. Her older brother's death weighed heavily on her mind and she had been reduced to a mental pulp for over four months since the funeral. Richard was everything to her: her muse, a father figure and the great magician in her life who would listen patiently to all her problems and then wave his hand like a wand and utter wise words like priestly incantations. He never failed to come to her rescue, to make things better.

Now, after years of terrible suffering he was gone. The void his death created in Hermione's life was almost unbearable.

She had lucid moments in which she plodded around the house silent and brooding, hardly speaking. Her mother worried about her, but in many ways she was part of the problem. Dealing with someone as sensitive as Hermione needed a character like her brother Richard, a natural patient intellect, not someone irascible and bad tempered. Besides, Hermione lost respect for her mother when she found a stash of gin bottles located in various corners of the house. She suspected that the intake of gin predated Richard's death by a decade at least. Now, it was the only way her mother could cope, but it left little or no support for Hermione. She recalled, tearfully, that even when he was clearly suffering and in pain, almost up to the very end, Richard always tried to make everything right, urging her to understand her mother more.

Tonight, Hermione's head spun with fatigue and emotion and she believed that her gloom would never end. She contemplated suicide several times, but had neither the courage nor the will to carry it out, but she knew in her heart that this was a cry for help rather than a realistic option. It was certainly true that she had always been a drama queen since her childhood. When things didn't go her way sulks and tantrums were the order of the day and dear, dependable Richard would intervene, invent a story with her, and they would act it out in the privacy of her room. But now he would never do that again.

She moved her hot feet out of the bedclothes only to retreat because they got cold, then she rolled on her stomach, turning onto her back minutes later. Putting her hands to her head she wiped away the tears. As she turned over, she heard a high pitched sound, not a ring as such, it was more like a whine or a howl. The light from the moon shining through the window caught her eyes as its rays shafted through the net curtains like silver spears, highlighting her toes as if they were ten silhouetted Mandarin shadow dancers.

To her amazement, she saw through a crack in the curtains the figure of a large dog, like a wolf, crossing the fence-line in the garden. It turned its head towards her house, stopped, then circled for a while before walking towards the window more slowly, head hung low, eyes white and looking straight at her. The shadow got larger and Hermione felt her heart race as she realised it was heading directly towards her room. She was transfixed and couldn't move a muscle, although all her senses wanted her to get up and run.

The howling stopped and she became aware of a scratching at the windowsill and realised to her horror that the window was open wide. Her mind raced and for a second or two, fear filled her stomach. All of a sudden, bathed in moonlight, the face of a beautiful wolf came to the window. Its crown was dark blue grey and there was a hint of thin black eyebrows above sparkling, almond shaped eyes. The face was white and so was the collar and chest, and the rest of the fur was a mixture of grey and brown with some beige flecks. But, it was the eyes that were the most striking feature. They had an intelligent, compassionate, expressiveness about them. She felt that they were piercing her soul, as frightened as she was, this mesmerised and calmed her. Strangely, fear completely disappeared and she was left with a sense of being protected and looked after. They stared at each other for a while then the wolf jumped over the window sill and through the net curtains trotting over to her bed, which it then lay beside. After a while, she tentatively reached out and touched the animal's fur and it felt light, fluffy and silky.

40

Hermione breathed more easily, her heart stopped racing and gradually, she fell asleep to the feel of the wolf's heartbeat as she stroked its chest. She slept more deeply that night than she had for months.

Malvern is typical of any small English rural town. Its market square is paved with neat blocks, has numerous park benches and small tasteful statues commemorating the actions of founding fathers, religious characters and other worthy citizens. Its old market cross marked the place where people would meet and talk, buy and sell goods, as they had done for hundreds of years. Today was Saturday and people were walking about, talking and smiling as they looked at goods on sale at the various colourful market stalls. Hermione walked slowly through the town, breathing deeply and looking up at the sunshine; she hadn't felt this good for a long time. She thought that perhaps she had at last turned the corner in her grieving.

When she arrived back at her home in Lime Street, she noticed the door was open and heard her mother's frantic and high-pitched voice in the back room and thought she was talking to herself again. Then she heard the chink of glass against bottle and her stomach knotted as the realisation dawned on her that her mother was knocking back the gin.

Hermione stood in the hallway, dejected and not really wanting to enter the lounge. Quite suddenly, out of the shadows, a tall female figure appeared in front of her and she jumped with fright. At first, it seemed to look straight through her, then their eyes met and she was unable to move her gaze. The woman spoke first, her voice elegant and soothing.

"Hello, I've just seen a nice room, it's really quite cheap. I mean the one that is two doors down from the bathroom upstairs. I understand that the rent covers all electricity, but not breakfast and I agreed to take my meals elsewhere. That's fine because I don't really eat very much."

The woman towered over her and sounded so 'matter of fact'. As they shook hands she continued to look directly at Hermione. She was breathtakingly attractive, but most stunning of all was the long leather coat with a grey fur collar she was wearing. It was a strange garment to wear on a mild day in May.

"You must be Hermione. Your mother has told me all about you. I'm Ursula, very pleased to meet you."

Hermione noticed the flash of white teeth as Ursula smiled and felt a sudden warmth flood through her body.

"How do you do," she said, then she realised she was being formal. "Oh, I am sorry, how boring of me. Hello, yes, I'm Hermione, nice to meet you. Are you to stay here then?"

"Yes, your mother wanted to rent your brother's room rather than, well, leaving it empty. I am so sorry by the way, so very sorry. Your brother sounds the most marvellous person, it was such a shame."

Hermione replied quickly, as she had done when dozens of other condolences were passed to her. "Thank you, we are never really going to get over it, we just need some time that's all."

She turned and looked towards the stairs. "It will be nice to have another person around, I had no idea Mummy was looking for a lodger."

Hermione formed a firm friendship with Ursula. She came back from her job at a local insurance agent's office each day and together they would meet on the patio, by the rose trees and talk about almost every subject imaginable. Whatever Hermione wanted to discuss, Ursula knew something about, but amazingly, only enough to get Hermione talking. And talk she did, endlessly, over and over. It sometimes felt as though she was emptying an enormous intellectual reservoir that was full to bursting point. Although Hermione told her a lot about her life, Ursula was much less forthcoming, deftly avoiding questions about her past or the present. Over the next few months, Hermione found her even more of an enigma. Despite that, she enjoyed her company and felt an immediate kinship. She loved their walks around the town as the sun was setting and darkness falling – they never walked in the day time - it was almost as if they were patrolling the area like two Victorian policemen. Back in her room she couldn't help thinking that it sometimes seemed as though Ursula was on a mission. There was a sense of urgency and energy that was quite daunting at times and yet Hermione never really knew what she did for a living. Questions were parried away with the skill of a professional lightweight boxer. So Hermione gave up probing.

Sometimes, Hermione would hear Ursula pacing around her room at all hours. Up and down, endlessly. The steps would occasionally stop, as if Ursula was thinking about something, then off she would go again. On one occasion, she even thought that she heard the sound of the window being slowly opened. Ursula would apologise profusely when they met the following day, usually in the early evening, and explain that she often had bouts of insomnia. That was the only time that Hermione could catch her, since she never seemed to be around during the day, or at breakfast.

It was another indifferent Saturday and after Hermione had collected cash from the bank for housekeeping, she went to her favourite coffee shop on the High Street, ordered an Americano and biscuits, and sat watching the world go by. The previous night many of the old bad dreams had returned. Perhaps it was the knowledge that the following day would be tinged with sadness. It was only a small thing, but Richard's favourite soccer team, Tottenham Hotspur, had reached the final of the European Cup and Hermione's eyes watered as she thought how her brother would have cheered and punched the air. In the last two years before he died, he was too weak for that, but in his earlier days he would have yelled like a crazy boy.

Her coffee was strong and hot, and she sipped it loudly. Sensing someone was watching her she looked up and saw Ursula standing to the side of her table smiling.

She jumped with fright.

"Feeling low?"

"Good grief, Ursula, where did you come from?"

Ursula smiled a now familiar big smile without parting her lips then said, "Aha, wouldn't you like to know?"

She reached down and touched Hermione gently on the nose like a big sister would.

Hermione ordered a glass of water for Ursula and the waiter looked surprised. He brought it to her, placing it on the table immediately in front of her.

'How stupid was that,' she thought and huffed loudly, pushing the glass towards Ursula on the other side of the table.

Ursula smiled and seemed unconcerned as she caught the exchange between Hermione and the waiter. "I don't think he saw me, my dear. But, it's good to get your own way, you know. You haven't had enough of that, have you? Control. Ah yes, control. So often, we dream of control, but rarely does anyone get the chance to really take it and enjoy it. Mostly, you exist in a kind of, well a state of confusion, like that man in Franz Kafka's novel, TheTrial, what's his name?"

Hermione sat open mouthed. They shared so many of the same interests it was uncanny.

"Josef K, but my God, Ursula, why did you think of him? I had a bad dream last night, it was pretty awful. I was lost in a grey building full of endless corridors, dull lighting and doors that opened into more endless corridors. Then I met him, you know, poor old Josef. He was sitting on a metal chair with his head in his hands, sobbing, saying he was a failure to himself and his father, in fact everyone. His cries made me feel awful. I turned and ran, because somehow I felt that whatever he was suffering was afflicting me too. The trouble was that I found it difficult to get out of the building no matter which way I turned or how far I ran. There were endless corridors and doors. I woke up in a real sweat. It was weird and frightening, believe me."

Ursula just sat looking at Hermione and didn't say anything. Hermione felt uneasy and reached across the table for the glass of water, took a large swallow and then put it back in front of Ursula. For some strange reason she knew that she had to continue, it was almost as if Ursula's silence was encouraging her to tell more.

"But, there was something else," Hermione's voice faltered.

"Tell me more," said Ursula. Her voice had that tone that seemed to already know what Hermione was going to say and Hermione felt childish in her shadow.

"It's silly," she said, looking around the now empty coffee shop, "you'll only laugh".

Ursula smiled. "Go on, you must tell me everything, absolutely everything."

44

Hermione took a deep breath and felt strangely excited, stupid and at the same time quite silly.

"Well, in the dream, I found myself agitated and in a sweat, running down long corridors in a large concrete building, but couldn't find my way out. But then I heard the sound of laughing and came across a large double door. As I turned to go inside I saw a beautiful blue pool bounded by several large stone pillars and coloured glass windows on either side of the room. There were six young men, and two more standing on the side of the pool. They were dressed in an assortment of bathing gear and were...well, very handsome." She looked down at the table.

Ursula laughed.

"Please don't make fun of me?"

"I'm not making fun of you. It sounds rather nice that's all. Were they - nice?"

She smiled and raised an eyebrow – Hermione blushed.

"I haven't known many boys, men I mean and I wanted to just keep looking at them. Most of my life has been looking after my mother and then Richard and I haven't had experience, in that way, you know..."

She paused for a moment, looked perturbed and shook her head. "It was so stupid – so surreal. Anyway, the boys shouted and urged me to go into the pool and I walked into the water fully clothed. It felt really quite cool as I went in deeper. I had to, you see, the only door out of the building was on the other side of the pool. When I was in the pool, the boys were laughing at me. Not doing anything just laughing at me and I felt so stupid. I had to struggle through the water to get away from their mocking."

There was more silence.

"Oh, poor Hermione. The figures, the boys that is, they were your conscience that's all. You should've reached out to them, you know, touched them," she smiled and her eyes lit up. "I mean, tried to get to know them, wouldn't you have liked that?"

Hermione looked agitated and blurted. "I don't know, I really don't know. But what does it mean?"

"Hermione, this dream reflects what you've missed over the years. They are young men and you are an attractive young woman

45

and you should be able to influence them. But you don't know how to control men, in fact they may as well be Martians for all you know, because you don't know how to relate to them. You're introverted and dare I say it, guilty."

Hermione stirred the remains of her coffee. "I suppose so. But guilty of what?"

Ursula reached out and touched her hair and although she liked it Hermione moved away self-consciously.

"Dear me, Hermione, don't pull away so, I want to help you, not seduce you. Since you ask, guilty of having a good time and letting yourself go."

Hermione put her fingers to her lips and nervously laughed.

Ursula stood up and inclined her head towards the Malvern Hills. Without saying a word Hermione followed her out of the café, leaving more than enough cash for the coffee and water.

The waiter came over to the table, picked up the money and watched Hermione walking down the road alone - he shook his head.

The Malvern Hills are especially beautiful in the late spring and small white fluffy clouds drifted aimlessly across the horizon in front of the low sun. It was a short drive to an area known as the British Camp. Walking had been Hermione's only way of retreating into herself and today it was rather special that she was able to share her bad dream with Ursula. Ursula, who was so enigmatic, yet patient and understanding, and now assumed the role of guide and mentor. As they walked along the grassy path around the rim of the hills, she studied her features. Long brown hair, sleek long nose and when she looked at you, piercing eyes. And that coat, always that coat.

After sitting quietly on a large rock for a while, Ursula stood up abruptly.

"I think it's about time we liberated you, Hermione," she said.

"What do you mean?"

"Well, what do you do for fun?"

"This is my fun, Ursula, this, just talking to you. Believe you me, sometimes it's just what I need."

Ursula cocked her head to one side.

"You have led a sheltered life. Follow me. Let's release the real you." Ursula walked on and Hermione had to almost run to keep up.

When they got back to the car Ursula directed Hermione to drive to nearby Gloucester. They hardly said a word and after an hour they reached the outskirts of the town. Ursula navigated her through several narrow streets and eventually asked her to stop outside a café. It was called Café Minos. It was badly decorated on the outside and the windows needed cleaning. Curtains were hung, European-style, with the centre of the material higher in the middle than the sides, so that the inside of the cafe could be seen from the street.

"Okay, in you go and ask for, 'something special'," said Ursula.

"What," Hermione spluttered. "Do you mean what I think you mean?"

"Yes."

"But, that's…"

Then Ursula interjected. "Oh dear, years of being little 'Miss Innocent'. Listen to me, go in and do as I tell you. You deserve this Hermione. You deserve it."

Ursula leaned back and half-smiled at her. "Remember when you looked through your mother's photographs and found those of her topless with her boyfriend? And the one where she was wearing a mini-skirt so short you could see her knickers? She may have lost her looks now Hermione, but she had a life, had a lot of fun and lived it to the full, I can assure you of that. You deserve to have a chance of that too. Besides, one little snort of something hardly amounts to a lifetime's debauchery. Be good to yourself for once. Go on now."

Hermione thought for a moment, smiled slowly and stood up.

"Yes, you know something, I think I do. I bloody well do."

She got out of the car and for some reason locked it. Then she looked back at Ursula's image behind the windscreen that smiled and waved her on. Laughing nervously, she went inside the café.

Entering the café, Hermione wondered how Ursula had known about her finding the photographs of her mother. Perhaps the two of them had also shared some time together? That was strange, because her mother never acknowledged Ursula's existence. She probably just took the money for the gin.

As she sat down at the far end of the café she remembered how shocked she had been to see her mother in the photographs. It was difficult to relate the carefree adolescent with the haggard sop that went to pieces after Hermione's father left the family home. But at least her mother had a youth worth speaking about.

A young woman dressed in black wearing a small dirty grey apron approached her, with a notebook in her hand. She had short brown hair and wore a headband made out of red material. Her face was almost white and expressionless so that her painted red lips and the unusually large nose became the most prominent features.

"Coffee please, and er, I'd like," Hermione looked embarrassed and said in a somewhat lower voice, "something special."

The waitress gave a look of gentle recognition and glanced around the café. Then after a few moments she went to the counter and poured a coffee, bringing it back to the table. She put it down and then left without a word.

Hermione drank the coffee and saw the waitress talking to a man in the shadows of the room behind the counter and they both stared at her for a while. After about ten minutes the waitress came to her table and placed a receipt on a plate in front of her. When the flap was turned over it showed a scrawled price: fifty-five pounds. Under the receipt was a small cellophane packet of white powder. Without demur, Hermione took out the correct cash and placed it on the table. The waitress quickly scooped it up and walked away without speaking. Hermione put the packet into her pocket, finished her coffee and walked out of the café.

What had she done? She felt excited, liberated and in control. It felt so good. It was like walking on air, like the first time she had skipped a class at school and no one noticed, or pocketed some liquorice without the shopkeeper catching her.

Back in the car she drove away laughing, because she had never done anything really illegal like this before. But where was Ursula? After no longer than a minute a voice from the back of the vehicle startled her.

"Smart girl, now stop and let's get you snorting some 'heaven dust'."

Hermione jumped. "Where did you get to?"

Ursula laughed. "Never mind, just park and do as I say."

Then they both made piggy noises and giggled like schoolgirls.

The car stopped next to a fairground and after trial and error Hermione managed to snort up all the powder, then lay back and let it take her. It felt good. So good that she wanted to go to the fairground, just like she had with her father and Richard. She recalled all the noise and music, the sounds of the bumper-cars, shooting a rifle and throwing hoops to win a teddy bear. She felt tremendously happy and light-headed.

Hermione got out of the car, laughing to herself uncontrollably and stumbled through the car park into the fairground. The lights were bright and sparkling. The noise was deafening and all the shapes around her moved in a fluid kind of way as though they were made of jelly. Then she saw something that made her heart skip a beat. It was a carrousel. Oh, how she loved to ride those horses round and round, with the wind in her face and the music loud in her ears.

Soon she was up onto a horse and she stuffed some paper money in a surprised young boy's hand as he came around asking for fares.

"That should keep me on the ride for some time," she thought.

The large plaster and wood horse felt good as she hung on to its neck, grasping its body with her thighs, leaning forward and kissing its mane. Then off they went and memories began to tumble out of her mind. She saw her father, a cheeky kind of chap, casually dressed in a blue check shirt and black jeans, smiling at everyone and giving Richard money to spend. Then she saw Richard in a familiar scene, always giving Hermione half of everything he had, ducking around stalls and pointing his fingers at her like a cowboy, firing imaginary shots at her. Pow! Kepow! Lovely Richard always laughing, lovely father always smiling.

Round and round they went. She looked to one side and was surprised and yet amused to see Ursula on a separate horse, not on, but off the carrousel – how the hell did she do that? Ursula smiled and waved. Who cares anyway? What fun she was having. What a release of energy and happiness. After a while she was dizzy with laughing and all the noise, but then to her surprise she noticed that her horse had also left the carrousel. It was gliding through the air and eventually moved up and over the fairground, circling the city until it fell slowly through a mist to the ground, stopping outside a large grey building. She shuddered and felt helpless, yet strangely elated.

It was the building of many corridors in her nightmare.

She was afraid at first to go in, and yet felt compelled to do so. Ursula's voice came from inside, gently coaxing her in, urging her to confront her fears. Now the horse had become real and it pawed the ground and nuzzled her, as if it too was encouraging her to enter the building. Holding the reins, she went inside. As she walked she felt the ground wobble under her feet so that at times it was difficult to keep a steady balance, it was a bit like walking on a waterbed. On and on she went, until through the dim, greenish, misty light she came across a window on the left side of the corridor.

Rubbing away some of the dust she bent forward and looked through it. What she saw made her gasp: it was her mother. Transfixed, she could do no more than watch the scene in front of her. It was an exact black and white facsimile of the photographs she found in her mother's cupboard, the ones Ursula had described. The only difference was that the scene was not still, but moving, with all the characters laughing and joking. Her mother was topless and wearing tight jeans, she had a blue headband and was holding a lighted cigarette that was oddly shaped and looked home made. Hermione watched her as she kissed first one boy, then another. Then she puffed at her cigarette and three young men hugged her all at once. She laughed and hugged them back and to Hermione's horror allowed them to fondle her body and slowly they started to remove her jeans. Her chest burst with anxiety and she wanted to scream, but she couldn't. It was her mother – her mother of all people, behaving like a tart. She was confused and wondered whether she was upset or jealous, or perhaps both.

The floor still wobbled under her feet and she managed to stagger away, breathless and eyes full of tears, towards another window a few yards away. She had long since dropped the reins to the horse, but it followed obediently. There was a throbbing sound in her head and she could hardly concentrate. Despite that, she looked through the next window and her spirits rose as she called out to a gangly young man dressed in a polo shirt and jeans in a garden of bright flowers on the other side. Her heart leapt.

"Richard, Richard it's me!"

Her beautiful brother was standing some way away on the left of the window, handsome, smiling and beneath his cotton shirt with the sleeves rolled up, he appeared tanned and well toned. When she was a young girl, she had peeked through the keyhole once and watched him strip wash and marvelled at his manly physique. Now there he was, his smile radiated outwards and towards her, brightening her world. Then for no reason, he frowned a little and turned abruptly to his right and walked slowly across the setting. The whole series of images took on the form of a kind of grainy, sepia coloured cinematography, fluttering as one image changed to another. As he moved to the right, he appeared to grow progressively weary and his features aged terribly with his every step. A terrible anxiety gripped her. Eventually, she saw him reach his bedroom in the family home. He lay down and then half sat up, reaching out his hand towards her, calling her name. By now his hair was almost gone, with a few grey wisps remaining, and his face was haggard and lined. He didn't look young any more.

"Hold on, Richard, hold on," she choked as she banged her hands on the window. The tears came again and so did all the painful memories of looking after him as he slowly died.

After a few moments the images cleared leaving the window empty and she stumbled on down the corridor, tears streaking down her face. Another window came into view and she dreaded what she would see. But this time it was clear glass and she saw a picture of herself and her one and only boyfriend as they sat on their last date in a restaurant. This had been a patient, long term affair, worthy of more attention by her. She watched as they sat and ate a meal in silence and then halfway through, she got up and said a few words to the boy and left, her knife and fork still forming a 'V' on the plate of half finished food. He sat there for a while and then pulled out a small box and opened it. In it was a ring. Then she saw him throw it into a nearby waste bin and leave. He looked dejected. She felt a terrible dull pain in her chest, the kind you get when you badly let someone down and there is no going back. But it couldn't be helped.

Was it because he couldn't measure up to Richard or that Richard now needed her more?

Her head was aching with the throbbing and she found it difficult to stand still because of the wobbling floor. The horse neighed loudly as if warning her and she noticed a hand outstretched through a nearby window beckoning her onwards. When she reached the window she felt a sudden wave of revulsion at what she saw. It was the image of the philosopher Nostradamus sitting at a secretaire close to the window. Paper scrolls lay all over the place and several quill pens were stacked near a large ink bottle. She recognised the image because she had cut it out and put it into her scrapbook when she was eleven years old. Nostradamus was wearing voluminous linen mustard coloured breeches, a white cotton shirt and dirty red velvet waistcoat, covered by a large blue cloak. He wore a five-cornered hat over straggly greasy hair. His beard was matted and badly trimmed, and his eyes were wide and bloodshot.

"I've done your prediction Hermione. You want to see it my girl?" He said in a tone that seemed to mock her. "Not like the other worldly stuff I produced. Yours is full of nice juicy guilt."

"But that's stupid, I've got nothing to be guilty about?" she blurted.

"Not guilty, but guilt: G-U-I-L-T, you stupid girl. You know what I mean, that pervasive stuff that fills your body and soul and rots from within? That which prevents you from having a life, remember? It's all here Hermione," his hand hit the parchment in front of him. "All here for you to read. Poor Richard, your spiritless alcoholic mother who drove your father out of the home, your one and only boyfriend and of course, your inhibited sexuality, Hermione. Everything is covered - lots of lovely guilt."

He began to laugh maniacally and suddenly reached out for her and she recoiled, falling over, then getting up and staggering away from the window and all its horrors. She heard his manic laughter and her head throbbed wildly. Everything that he said struck a blow to her heart and she stood with her hands to her head, eyes closed.

After a short while, she became aware of a voice singing gently. It was hers. It came from the last window in the long corridor and she walked, shaking, towards it. There she saw her image, standing in front of the bathroom mirror at home, slowly disrobing. She watched apprehensively as the image removed the final items of clothing and stopped to look in the long mirror. It was a faint but frequent memory – something she did before she relaxed after a hard day working, running the house and looking after her mother, and then her sick brother Richard. She remembered the familiar ritual, with the door locked and the keyhole blocked up with tissue paper. Her doppelganger got into a warm soapy bath and lay there for a while, wide-eyed, sad looking, staring at the ceiling with glassy eyes. Hermione's heart skipped a beat, her heart sank and she flushed recalling what came next.

"Oh, stop, the window," she shouted, embarrassed at the scene, and tried frantically to rub steam and water over it to obscure the image. Impossibly, the window appeared to get bigger and bigger as she looked at it. How was this happening?

Sounds of voices in the corridor filled the air and to her horror she looked up and saw that the characters had left their windows and were coming towards her. Her mother and the boys she had been dancing with, Richard, Hermione's boyfriend, even Nostradamus who fallen out of his window, were laughing and mocking her. This made her frightened and upset. They mustn't see her in the bath. She turned to bang on the window to attract the attention of her image, but recoiled. The window had grown to twice the size. It was impossible for her to block the pictures and when she tried, the window scene just moved along the corridor towards the people coming towards her. They continued to laugh and point at the scene. As she ran up to the window, it simply moved on faster. When she finally caught up with it, it changed direction, then size, then moved back to its original position and no matter how she tried, it eluded her. All the time the characters laughed hysterically and pointing at her image.

Eventually, she fell to her knees sobbing with humiliation, frustration and anger. Her mother's hurtful tone could be heard mocking her and her boyfriend who once loved her was shouting at her. Then she saw Richard, who was not laughing. He just stood there and seemed to be the only one who understood everything. Then the crowd of fools, danced and bumped into his prostrate body, they overran him as he fell to the ground, his body slowly turning into green dust as they trod all over him.

She screamed.

Just as she thought she could take no more horror, her vision slowly disappeared. The world went grey and she saw a single white light ahead. Then she felt the ground wobble underneath her for the last time, before unseen hands lifted her body as if to the sky.

Then nothing.

Hermione's mother woke up with a start, her bedclothes in a bundle around her. Her head was thick with the red mist of alcohol induced depression. She swallowed some Prozac prescribed for her by her general practitioner, but this rarely did any good, so she resorted to more gin. Her mouth felt thick and treacly and she coughed to clear her throat. She had long since given up on her daughter's behaviour, but this last episode had taken the biscuit. Drugs. Of all things, drugs. Not like harmless spliffs when she was young, but cocaine. What a fool.

The world was a painful enough place to live in. As if she hadn't had enough to put up with, what with her feckless husband, the sad death of dear Richard and then, when all she wanted was a good loving daughter, the girl constantly rambled and talked to herself like some demented parrot.

The ambulance crew had been very kind and helped her get Hermione to her bed. She fell off a carousel so they said. What kind of way was that to behave at her age? That was three days ago. It was a short walk to the toilet, but her legs were weak and unsteady, so she held onto the wall as she tottered down the corridor. Three days and not a word from the stupid bitch.

Walking along the corridor she passed Hermione's bedroom on the left. The door was still ajar. The window was open and the curtains flapped in a light breeze. The bed was only slightly rumpled, turned down and empty.

She winced wearily. "She ups and leaves the house. God knows where she's gone. More trouble - more problems. Well she can come back when she likes or stay away, it's all the same to me. No more police or ambulances. That's it, finished. No bloody more."

The toilet door slammed shut and the seat creaked and slipped slightly to the side as she sat on it.

High in the Malvern Hills, as the evening drew in and light dimmed, a low howling sound rode on the wind. A she-wolf, sat looking down on the town, imperious and regal in stature. It looked to one side for a moment and its lips drew back in a smile. There, squirming in the damp night grass was a younger wolf, also a female, rolling on her back, legs in the air enjoying the coolness of the night. After a few moments she came over to the older wolf and nuzzled her neck. They bent their heads together and gazed into each other's eyes.

Moments later, when the moon began to lose its light as a cloud wrapped it in an embrace, a light went on in a bedroom in one of the many small houses that back onto the hills. A sound of sobbing could be heard coming from a bedroom, which was the source of the light. It was a sob from someone hopeless, deflated and beaten. It held the two wolves spellbound and begged for attention.

After listening to it for a while, the older animal looked at the younger one and they flashed their eyes at each other in mute agreement. Moments later they trotted down the hill towards the source of the misery.

Luckily, the bedroom was on the ground floor and the window was open.

# INTERSTELLAR HIGHWAY

Rebecca closed the door to her sister's cottage with a bang and strode purposefully down the path, slamming the gate equally loudly as she left the garden. She put both her arms on the roof of her red convertible 1983 Lancia sports car and took a deep breath, exhaling the warm mist into the cold night air. The weekend with her sister had not gone well at all and they left each other, hearts beating, tight-lipped and full of hurt. Geraldine was the sweetest person in the world and yet for some unknown reason their egos sometimes collided and when this happened the effect was volcanic. Perhaps it was inevitable. Each had travelled the route from mid twenties to just over thirty, establishing their lives professionally and with partners, unwittingly vying for attention and trying to get one step further on than the other.

She put her leather overnight bag into the boot, opened the car door, got in and sat down heavily in the sports seat and as she did so, rainwater from the soft-top splashed her face and she brushed it aside irritably. The leather upholstery felt cold on her bottom and she threw her coat onto the small back seat. After sitting still for a moment she reached into the glove compartment for a small tin box that contained several roll-up cigarettes. It wasn't the wisest thing to do, but lighting up a cannabis spliff was what she now really craved. Old university-habits die hard. As she inhaled the soothing aromatic smoke, she noticed the bedroom light in her sister's cottage go out. Smoke filled her lungs and she held it there for a short moment before exhaling - it felt good – closing her eyes, tears of frustration welled up.

Her sister infuriated her and drove her to the limit of her patience, yet despite this there was a strong bond between them and she loved her without question. But in situations like today, she needed some space to cool down.

After a while she finished the cannabis cigarette, threw the butt into the road and turned the key in the ignition. The engine burst into life. It had a powerful yet soft rumble to it, displaying strength of engineering with the subtlety of Italian sex appeal. As the car pulled away, Rebecca took out her mobile telephone and put it into the special holder on the mahogany dashboard – it flashed brightly as it received a small charge of electricity. The tyres skidded on the gravel as the car sought traction then, gripping the surface, the Lancia accelerated gracefully and she felt a slight force in the middle of her back as it did so.

The shortcut to the motorway was via several small, narrow roads just about wide enough for one and a half cars. Tonight the trees either side of the road seemed to dip inwards, eerily reaching to the car. It spooked her and she regretted not taking the longer route via the main road. To make matters worse there was a thickening mist that almost obscured the road ahead. It was an hour before midnight and she had at least a two-hour drive home. Eventually, she saw a dimly lit blue and white sign indicating the M25 and turned down the slip road and onto the motorway. As soon as she got onto the M25 she settled down for the short drive to the turnoff for the A3 and the long journey home to Portsmouth.

After a while she felt a strange, throbbing headache come on and regretted her puffs of cannabis, it was so bad that she considered stopping briefly, but it was late and she thought better of it.

All of a sudden the headache passed and as it did so, the mist took on a strange hazy, bright blue-purple tinge and she noticed that from time to time there were small flashes of light as though somebody was taking flash photographs. Narrow coloured beams of light sporadically flashed then exploded like starburst fireworks. Rebecca thought it was the result of an expensive birthday party celebration.

Unperturbed, her thoughts remained with her sister Geraldine. She had always looked up to her and envied her clever mind. Rebecca was the skilful one, quick to learn IT skills, feisty and realistic and she was good at reading situations. On the other hand, Geraldine lived in a classical world of paper tigers, drama and literature and wouldn't see a charging elephant until she felt its breath on her neck and even then she would probably offer it a bun. How could you get mad with such a person? Rebecca felt remorseful. She berated herself for being so hard-headed at times, and even began to question her own view that it was part of her character and that was all there was to it. Anyway, it takes two to change, why the heck should she do all the work?

"Oh, why do you make me so mad!" she said out loud.

Seconds later, she noticed a car undertaking on the inside lane. That irritated her immensely and she looked up to catch the driver's eye in order to give him or her, an admonishing glare. As she did so she flinched with fright. The car was a large black American Buick with lots of shiny chrome and ostentatious fins on the back. Driving it was a man wearing a large white cowboy hat with silver studs around the centre and his head was down so far on the steering wheel that she couldn't make out his face. His whole body was hunched over the wheel as though he was concentrating hard on just driving straight ahead like crazy.

Just as Rebecca strained to get sight of the driver, he looked up and her chest instantly tightened at what she saw. She could just make out a white heavily creased face with blazing red eyes that seemed to actually shine. He then turned his attention back towards the road ahead and accelerated away into the distance. She asked herself whether she was fantasising. Was that real? It must surely be a man in fancy dress.

Rebecca tried to make sense of the fleeting image. She didn't feel scared, just incredulous as she watched the rear lights of the large vehicle disappear in front of her. Blinking a few times, she cleared her eyes and peered through the rain and mist. The Buick seemed to be jet propelled it travelled so fast. It was most odd.

Then there were more flashes of light, from the left and right and sometimes high in the sky. She began to feel irritable. Where the hell was the turn-off for the A3, she had been driving for ages and yet had seen no signs whatever? Something was distinctly wrong.

Her mobile telephone flashed and before she could reach for it the speaker came on automatically and a high-pitched voice, with a strange accent addressed her.

"Good evening, you are approaching junction twenty-three on the interstellar highway. You cannot take this junction. Please drive carefully. Thank you."

"What the…?" she thought. "How…?"

Her heart beat faster as a junction appeared and she tried to turn the steering wheel to leave the motorway, but it wouldn't budge. Even the accelerator and brake were inoperable. She felt helpless. This was crazy.

Suddenly, a silver-grey bullet shaped car overtook her like a rocket; she looked at her speedometer which was showing eight-five miles an hour, so what speed was that car doing?

Gripping the steering wheel tightly she tried to concentrate on her situation. What the hell was happening? She was powerless in a car that wouldn't respond.

As if all that was not crazy enough, her eyes widened in surprise and shock when, completely out of nowhere she came upon a dozen American bison running in front of her in the same direction. On top of two of them sat Sioux Indians full-feathered headdress. Frightened out of her wits she tried to pull the wheel hard to the left then the right. This time the car responded and she shrieked with fright as her Lancia narrowly missed hitting the large beasts. She eventually passed them and noticed the bison had red bloodshot eyes and saliva was falling from their mouths in great white globules – they must have been travelling at least at sixty miles an hour, how could this be?

The Sioux Indians, like the driver of the large Buick earlier were hunched forward, oblivious to anything but following the highway ahead. Their faces were contorted and they concentrated hard on the task of driving their bison forward.

Rebecca was in a state of shock. Was there a circus in the area? Were they all high on drugs or something? This was a nightmare – she was convinced she would never, ever, touch cannabis again. The Bison disappeared behind her as her car drove on past them at high speed, through the mist and rain, accompanied by flashes of light, this time orange and green. She was very scared.

Fidor laughed as he looked at the screen and glimpsed Rebecca's shocked and frightened face. He sat in a large high-backed swivel chair, dwarfed within a cavernous area inside a cavity on a deserted asteroid, Star 4305. The area was the size of the Albert Hall and was surrounded by large metal cabinets covered with lights, flashing screens, pulsing nuclear and solar energy cells, cables and wires. A three-D image of Rebecca appeared on a large screen high up on the wall in front of him. He enjoyed frightening creatures from around the universe and his personally constructed interstellar highway was the best sport he had developed in a hundred time-spans. He chuckled at the antics of the American Indians riding the bison. That was funny, very funny, but not at all like the time that he had twenty elephants bumping into cars and trucks with their mahouts atop them, crouched in eternal fear, each whipping his beast for all he was worth, destined to ride the highway for eternity until their bodies rotted, the flesh falling off but the skeletons remaining fixed to their mission. He was especially proud of that concept, but was sad that the elephants had long since run themselves out, tiring and eventually being bumped off the highway by speeding vehicles.

Then his head jerked forward as someone slapped the nape of his neck hard. He looked up in surprise.

"Fidor, so this is what you have been up to," said his sister Granya. "I've been watching for the last time-span and I don't like what I see. You're cruel, Fidor, just like Federation said, but I didn't know you had created anything like this."

Fidor rubbed his neck and smiled at Granya.

"Dearest sister, when our parents allowed us to stay on planet Orama…"

Granya interjected furiously.

"No, Fidor, they exiled you, and me, because I was your sister remember?"

She glared at him.

"Yes, all right, have it your way, exiled. But we have all we need here and to all intents and purposes we are able to do as we please. And I have all this marvellous equipment to play with. I have so much fun."

He waved his arms at the array of equipment, screens and lights around him and laughed again.

Granya was not impressed and drove home her anger.

"But it's cruel and that's why you were sent here Fidor. You never change do you? If Mador finds out you will be in big trouble."

"He won't, dear sister, he won't. Now sit down and enjoy the show."

Fidor turned his attention to the screen and pointed a long bony finger at the image or Rebecca. "I particularly like this group of creatures. They are intelligent, very intelligent and they possess an enormous amount of emotion. This means that they are brave, courageous but, on the other hand, so much more easily frightened. It is so funny isn't it?"

Granya screwed her face up and bit her green lip. She had watched the earlier manoeuvre to transfer the hapless creature Rebecca from the M25 to the interstellar highway from behind a large cabinet in the corner, near the screen on the wall and realised what Fidor was up to. She despised her brother, but hated even more the ancient rules that had shackled her to his exile. She looked up at the screen and saw Rebecca's frightened face and felt sick inside.

Rebecca saw the mobile telephone flash again. It came on and a voice with high-pitched American twang spoke.

"Good evening, you are approaching junction twenty-four on the interstellar highway. You cannot take this junction. Please drive carefully. Thank you."

She raised her hand to her forehead, pinched the top of her nose as if to bring herself back to some kind of consciousness. Her body was sweating profusely, her hands felt clammy on the steering wheel and her feet had long since left the pedals, as the car seemed to speed on regardless.

As she tried to make sense of the utter madness of it all, a bright light appeared on her right. She looked around and saw to her horror a cadaverous corpse-like figure of an elderly man, his skin was yellow and taught against his skull, and his eyes were bulging. Wisps of remaining hair on his bald head stuck out untidily from the sides of his head. He was crouched over the wheel, the slightest sign that he was breathing was the white frothy bubbles that dripped profusely from the corners of his mouth. The figure turned slowly and looked at her, his forlorn, helpless expression begging her for help. Then, he resignedly returned his gaze to the road ahead and his vehicle accelerated away in a blaze of light, searching for a way out, a junction – something, anything!

Rebecca called on all her inner strength; she was not one to give in easily – it wasn't her way. Was this a cannabis-induced dream, or was it real? It was time to keep calm and think.

She reached for the mobile telephone and took it off the cradle. As she pressed the preset code for Geraldine, it lit up and startled her.

"This is the interstellar control. You are not allowed to contact anyone whilst on the interstellar highway. Please drive ahead and enjoy your journey. Thank you."

She held the phone close to her mouth and shouted at it.

"Stop, you idiot. I want to talk."

The mobile telephone remained live, but no voice came back to her. She convinced herself that she had made an impact on the voice and continued.

"What is going on? Are you controlling my car?"

There was only silence.

"If I am dreaming this then I will wake up and flush you down the toilet. If I am not and this is some kind of nightmarish situation which you are controlling, I'm here to tell you that you are a freak, you're pathetic, warped, do you understand me?"

By now she was angry and shouting. She put the phone back in the holder with a sharp thud and it flashed for an instant then went out.

Granya heard the whole exchange from the back of the hall, hidden in the shadows. She was glad that she hadn't been with Fidor when Rebecca shouted at him. When someone got the better of him he lost control of himself and that was always dangerous. That was why he was exiled. He had been considered dangerous to himself and to others in the community.

She had one slim chance to change things. Opening a small bag in front of her she brought out a round stone about three inches in diameter opaque and speckled with colours like a fire opal It shimmered brightly and piercing coloured shafts of light shot out from its surface. This was her only hope. It had been given to her by Midor and was to be used only in extreme situations. But first of all, she needed to get outside the metallic building, with its nuclear and solar power influences, to be able to use the stone effectively.

She would do it - it had to be done.

Rebecca felt tears welling up, just as they had when she had taken her first job and was bullied by a young male manager. She had rallied and gave as good as she got and she would do that now. Nothing frustrated her more than not knowing how to deal with a problem. Like her recent situation with her sister. Not being able to understand what was happening in their relationship, why they felt the way they did and why things went horribly wrong. But more than that, feeling that you have no influence over events unfolding at such a pace that you seem out of control and almost helpless.

Her anger was so great that she just wanted to get to the person behind the voice on her mobile telephone and rip his throat out.

Fidor laughed nervously and fidgeted with his controls.

"Female hell-creature. So you insult your controller do you? Well now you will regret that," he spat in anger.

Far behind him Granya was running into the darkness, between the tall metallic cabinets covered in flashing lights, her diaphanous robe flowing, tiny shards of light escaping from the round stone she clasped tightly in her fist.

Rebecca squinted into the mist and rain, and closed her eyes when flashes of light shot left and right. The car was cool but she still felt hot, her face flushed and red. She looked down and saw that her fingers were beginning to grip the wheel making her knuckles white. Then it dawned on her that she too was beginning to hunch over the steering wheel and quickly forced herself to sit up straight and avoid the crouch position. She wouldn't be cowed.

Rebecca jumped nervously when two vehicles shot past her narrowly missing the front end of her car and then moments later she only just avoided two tall, thin, human-like figures meandering along the centre of the highway, holding their heads in despair. Pumping the brake seemed to have some effect, but not a lot and when she tried to get the vehicle to slow down using the gears, it wouldn't respond.

Looking around she could see more vehicles coming towards her rear. In a small mini-Cooper on her left side, four skeletons rattled around the interior of the vehicle as it careered ahead at breakneck speed. One of the skeletons wore a baseball cap that had fallen forward and obscured one of the eye sockets giving it an incongruous, jaunty appearance.

On her right, seconds later, a Mercedes saloon swerved about as the driver, a woman with a crazed look on her face was trying to climb out of the car window. Some unseen force seemed to restrain her and she was screaming madly and pulling at her hair. Her face was contorted with fear and she seemed oblivious to the danger, concerned only with vacating the box prison of her vehicle. At one point she reached out and touched the side of the Lancia, her nails making a faint scratching sound - suddenly the Mercedes slowed and skewed off the road to her rear. There was a loud noise and a flash of explosive light.

Rebecca let out a small cry – would that eventually happen to her? No matter whether she crouched and drove for an eternity or fought back, was this to be her destiny?

The mobile telephone flashed and the voice came on again.

"Good evening, you are approaching junction twenty-five on the interstellar highway. You cannot take this junction. Please drive carefully. Thank you."

"Warped pig, bastard, mindless fool…" she shouted madly.

To her surprise, she felt good at shouting at the unseen person that seemed to be forcing her into this nightmare. Being defenceless is one thing, but giving that all-important 'V' sign, like a brave soldier about to be beheaded, in the face of terrible adversity, sat very neatly with her. She took her hands off the wheel and put them to her head. Why not? The car wouldn't divert from its track.

Was it her imagination, but did she hear someone laughing? Looking up, she saw a blaze of light appearing in her rear view mirror. A vehicle was behind her and flashing its lights wildly. She could do no more than try and see through the light to make out the danger. Astonishingly, the lights dimmed and the vehicle started to overtake. It slowed alongside her and as she looked up she recoiled in horror at what she saw. The vehicle was a large sedan with shiny silver fenders front and back shaped to look like teeth. Inside the sedan sat a large fat, shapeless green-fleshed creature, so big that the arms appeared short and squat against its frame that almost filled the vehicle. There was no discernable neck and its head seemed squashed into the body. The creature's face had pieces of green flesh hanging from it and the eyeballs protruded so much that they looked as though they would almost fall out. There was no noticeable mouth or nose. It looked straight at her and she felt its burning repulsive gaze. Her lower lip trembled. Now she was really scared and this was too much.

The vehicle dropped back behind her flashing its lights. It would surely hit her soon? Closer and closer it got until eventually it lightly bumped into the back of the Lancia. Her heart skipped a beat as the panic rose in her. Was he going to kill her? The car seemed to be positioning itself for another shunt.

As her heart beat faster and she braced herself for more to come, the mobile telephone flashed and she heard the voice with an American accent.

"Good evening, you are approaching junction twenty-six on the interstellar highway. You cannot _"

Then, to her surprise, the American voice was abruptly cut short. After a few seconds, a female voice, calmer and softer said, "_you *can* take the next junction, repeat, you *can* take the next junction, please do so quickly and drive carefully."

Rebecca's spirits rose in an instant and she didn't need telling twice. As she peered through the mist, falling rain and the flashing coloured lights she saw a junction come into view. A neon sign with the words, '*Here,*' ringed in flashing lights indicated the turnoff and she turned the steering wheel. It responded easily and so did the brake when she touched it to slow the vehicle down. The large sedan with its green monster driver overtook and sped past her.

The small slip road turned sharply to the left and she had to reduce her speed in order not to slide off the road. Her hopes of freedom were rising and she felt the elation of a prisoner being let free from a cell-block.

Soon she was back on a normal country road and for a time her body shook with relief at the normality of it all. Her mind was numb. She slowed the Lancia to take a bend and noticed a small lay-by, into which she instinctively turned and stopped. After cranking on the handbrake, she turned off the engine, stared ahead, then put her head on the steering wheel and cried. Although her fingers could hardly work properly, she sent a quick text message to her husband to say she was safe and not to worry. But it was impossible to go on, she was utterly exhausted, and she reached into the back of the car and grabbed a car blanket and her coat, then wrapped them around herself and settled down to sleep.

The sun was well above the horizon when Rebecca awoke from a four-hour nap, feeling enormously refreshed and surprisingly clear-headed. The drive home was uneventful and she felt strangely calm as the morning sun began to warm the car. She reached home and after parking went inside just as her husband Charles was preparing breakfast. He reached out to her and she gladly fell into his arms and told him of her emotional exchanges with her sister Geraldine and the turmoil her mind had been in, which had caused her exhaustion and the need to sleep in the car. He held her tight and, looking over her shoulder, smiled into the mirror at the other side of the room, because he had seen all this coming and expected the situation to boil over. Powerless, as most partners are, to intervene, he could only be there when she needed him most.

He loved Rebecca, but her major fault was that she never quite knew when to stand back from a discussion that was likely to generate an argument or disagreement, particularly when the other party carried a degree of baggage that might lead to misunderstandings - risk avoidance just wasn't in her vocabulary. But today, she looked strangely thoughtful.

Rebecca wanted to tell Charles she had smoked cannabis the night before and about the terrible horrific dream, for that was what it must surely have been. But it all seemed so very stupid. She would be certified insane if she told anyone - it was irrational, who would believe her? Besides, she had more to think about than a crazy dream and grabbed the digital telephone, hitting the 'preset' number for Geraldine.

Charles went to collect her overnight bag, just as she made contact with her sister. As he walked out of the front door, he heard words like, "sorry...me too...stupid...yes, of course I love you...never again..." and smiled broadly. Then he heard short giggles and peels of laughter.

He gathered Rebecca's bag from the car boot and made sure the Lancia's doors were locked; then something caught his eye. It was a small dent in the rear bumper, around which there were several flakes of silvery paint. Reaching down to wipe the flecks away, he was surprised when they quickly turned to dust as he brushed them off with his hand. He would certainly tease 'her ladyship' when the time was right - how on earth had she got a bump like that?

Granya sat with an elder as he tried to undo the damage of several time-spans by reprogramming equipment and shutting down power systems. But one programme was kept very much operational. She had taken the only action possible although it went against her beliefs and the rules of family, but it had to be done. Her eyes were full of tears as she looked up at the screen and saw her brother in a large grey and badly dented Cadillac. Fidor was sitting in the rear with several cadaverous creatures pawing at his face and body, as the vehicle careered at speed along an interstellar highway, through rain, mist and flashing lights, swerving around the debris of abandoned and crashed vehicles.

His eyes were bulging and he was screaming, but no one could hear his voice.

# SOULMATE

Ruth woke to the sound of her radio alarm and let the early morning strains of music and jabbering voices wash over her. She swung her legs over the edge of the bed and her toes dug into the soft pile carpet. It was an expensive woollen carpet, as were all the others in her exclusive penthouse flat overlooking the river Thames - the result of a successful career, achieved earned by spending most of her life at work.

Her six a.m. alarm was early by anyone's standards, but she had grown used to it. In business it was true that the 'early bird gets the worm', and she was always one step ahead of everyone else by the time they had reached their mid morning coffee.

Bathroom niceties were followed by the sound of the pulverising of the juicer. She was very organised and kept ingredients close to the machine so the process could be completed quickly and the result was fresh. Her cleaner had the awful task of throwing away the residue. To complete the process that kept a director-level woman at the top of her game, Ruth went for an early morning swim. Reaching the top of the executive ladder was important to her and she was determined to stay there, so keeping fit was a key ingredient of her success. She would never tire of this – getting the swimsuit on was the worst part, getting into the pool was sublime.

Several boyfriends had met an untimely end due to a worship of fast food and real ale and that was only first base. She set her sights high.

It was a short drive to the leisure centre. The day was cold and wet, the worst kind of morning, but typical of the period before Christmas, when people nostalgically prayed for snow which never came – only the rain. As she switched the engine off she heard a tap on the car window. It was Tim. He was ex-army, a really nice man, but did not have much else to commend him. Nice was never enough for Ruth. They had a friendly 'morning' relationship meeting regularly to swim before going to work, chatting about this and that.

She treated him politely, but was very careful never to raise his expectations.

"Hello, good morning and welcome to a dull day," she said.

Tim gave her a kind of 'I never give up' expression and said, "And, ma'am, better for having you grace it!"

She smiled back. "Bloody charmer!"

After changing, Ruth entered the pool area and stopped in her tracks. Tim was talking to a woman. They seemed happy and were laughing, together. For a moment she was full of envy. She had never seen this woman before and as she turned to go Tim looked over his shoulder at her, holding her gaze for a few seconds. It was a gaze that said, 'I would rather be talking to you this way.'

Or was that really the case? Was she feeling jealous – good grief, was she?

"What a lot of rubbish," she thought in annoyance, chastising herself and ignoring the leisure centre rules, she dived into the pool from the side and swam as far as she could under water. The lifeguards should have told her off, but it was a teenage boy and a girl and they were too busy flirting with each other.

After a good workout in the pool she showered, changed and went home. Ruth padded into the lounge, poured herself some freshly percolated coffee, sat down and spread the Times newspaper out in front of her, and scanned the business pages. She was the marketing director for a large tour company. The financial state of the nation was important to her and so was what was being peddled by her competitors. Keeping an eye on the wider economics was important. She was good at this and knew it.

On reflection, she had to admit that being at the top of the career tree could sometimes be lonely. Frowning, she flicked the pages noisily and tried to put the thought out of her mind. It was not her style to feel sorry for herself and she was convinced that it was better to be single. It would be nice to share her life, but she would never ever marry anyone unless she was absolutely sure that they were right for her. The problem was that she set the bar so high on almost every level that this was simply unattainable for any man. Moreover, she certainly wouldn't get hitched to satisfy her parents.

"Ah, parents," she thought, "they do worry."

She looked at her watch. Surprised at the time, she went to dress and left the mess for her cleaner to deal with. On leaving her penthouse suite, she looked across to Tower Bridge and the swirling water of the River Thames, brown and unfriendly in the winter light. Whilst waiting for the lift she turned towards a large panel hallway window and for a moment stood in front of its reflective surface and caught herself instinctively inspecting her image.

Half-smiling, she said out loud, "Nearly slim, nearly pretty and, damn it, nearly bloody forty! Oh well, at least the suit looks good."

Her day at the office was varied and interesting, as usual, but mainly because it was her mantra to take the lead in all things. There was a staff meeting, a board briefing and she had to motivate her senior managers to draft a product-marketing programme for the New Year. It was sometimes a chore to keep her staff focused, especially the juniors. They talked incessantly about parties and boyfriends and the excitement of approaching Christmas - all this wouldn't have been out of place in a junior school.

Ruth particularly disliked Christmas for a variety of reasons. It was no good her ignoring it though. Family presents had to be bought, an evening drinks session on Christmas Eve for her neighbours needed organising and of course, there was the inevitable office party. She felt like Scrooge, looked at the small mirror on her office and grimaced ghoulishly at herself.

"Oooooh, heavens, Miss!" said the registry lady, who had entered the office quiet and unseen, as she dropped the late post in her tray. Ruth blushed furiously.

"Oh, er, sorry. Wind...!" and she tapped her tummy.

The lady smiled politely and left the room.

Ruth saw the funny side. Perhaps she should be delighted at the effect it had on the lady – maybe she could wear that grimace during disciplinary meetings or her conversations with the managing director?

Her thoughts went back to Christmas. She still had to partake in the festivities and if nothing else she was a good partaker, in the general sense of having fun that was. But, in her case, and she desperately wondered why, at parties people always tried to match-make or fix her up with a partner. Did she look that desperate?

She swallowed hard recalling that some of their choices were beyond common sense. Sometimes she thought that friends and family would select almost anyone as long as it had male gonads, were unattached and warm. Every year, without fail, her Mum would take her into the kitchen and she knew what was coming.

"No mummy, no boyfriend yet; no mummy, time is not running out; yes mummy, I love my job!" She had to weather the same storm every Christmas, but she congratulated herself that she never ever let it spoil the festivities. Although it was irritating, in her heart she knew that her mum just wanted her to find a loving partner, just like her lovely dad.

Then there were the inevitable friends' dinners and parties. She knew she was good company and liked having fun. But she often had to avoid the inevitable randy boyfriend, or even husband, who thought the odd touch or cuddle, was in order to test the water. So flirting was most definitely out, because it was far too risky and sent mixed messages, experience taught her that much.

Ruth was jerked out of her thoughts by a knock on the door - it was one of the juniors.

"Come and join us, Miss Edgecombe. Marjorie is getting engaged!"

Ruth smiled and without a word left her desk and joined the junior walking towards an office desk that had been wildly decorated with paper flowers and balloons. It was Marjorie Ferris, fifty-something and widowed three years ago.

Marjorie looked at Ruth and they both smiled. They liked each other.

"You don't think Jack would mind, do you?" said Marjorie.

Ruth put her hand on Marjorie's shoulder.

"No, Marjorie, he wouldn't mind at all, he would've wanted you to be happy. He was that kind of guy."

She paused and looked to the heavens remembering Marjorie's religious nature and said with a smile, "He would say you shouldn't be alone and wish you good luck."

Marjorie was visibly grateful for the reassurance.

She smiled back at Ruth and said, "And you dear, you shouldn't be alone either if you don't mind me saying?"

Ruth was inured to the question and answered simply.

"No I don't mind and I know you mean well.  But it has to be 'Mr Right' "

"Okay, but don't wait too long, we are none of us perfect and you may be looking for someone who doesn't exist."

Ruth didn't answer and turned her attention to the decorations.

"So who did all this?" she said waving her arm at the displays.

A tall girl with glitter in her braided hair, wearing brightly coloured clothes and the biggest smile ever given to any human being came up to her and said in a confident and almost musical Jamaican accent, "Tha's me, girl."

Ruth looked at her before replying, ignoring the casual address 'girl'.  It was Eloise Sobers. She knew the girl by her reputation: upright and straightforward, good value, but sometimes strident to the point of rudeness. Oddly though, Ruth didn't care – she would take ten girls with character any day.

"Good work on the decorations Eloise. We should celebrate the spirit of Christmas and Marjorie's engagement. The champagne is on me in the Frog and Cucumber pub on the corner of Prince's Street," she said.

Eloise and the juniors smiled and cheered loudly, but the supervisor and manager gasped in surprise.

"But…but…the Franks' account?" they almost said in unison as the noise subsided.

Ruth captured the moment. "Look, it's four o'clock and we knock off at about six most days. We can celebrate tonight and," she turned theatrically to the staff, "it's up to you guys, but we can come in early all this week and make one hell of a push to finish this project, on time and with great quality. So, we can celebrate tonight. What do you say?"

The staff were now wound up and readily agreed with a cheer. The manager and supervisor blanched. All the same, it was important to reinforce the message. She turned to them and held up her hands for silence.

"I need your support though guys, this is an important marketing account that we really must win – do you understand that?"

Eloise responded loudly. "Yeah I hear you girl, regular good now, I'm up for dat, we'll all be there!"

Ruth smiled. She had hooked Eloise who would lead the herd. That meant the others would follow.

The remainder of the day went well and in cheery mood they later all set off to the Frog and Cucumber. Ruth was surprised to see that a good crowd had taken the opportunity to meet up together. Even those who did not usually drink in the evenings pitched up for a short while, to have fun and wish Marjorie much luck in her future union.

The impromptu party was soon in full swing and Marjorie was beaming from ear to ear and going as pink as the champagne. It is nice being happy, but even nicer sharing it with others. Ruth, usually tough at work, was letting her hair down a little and enjoying it. She was halfway through a smutty joke when she overheard Eloise say in the background, "Hey man, dat girl's cool."

A small gaggle of juniors seemed to nod in agreement. Then one of them added, "Yeah, she's tough sometimes. Probably because she's a woman at the top."

One of the others interjected. "On top, you mean…!" and they all shrieked with laughter at the implication. Another junior said, "Is that business before pleasure, or pleasure before business..." and there was more hysterical laughter.

Ruth did her best to ignore the joke and blushed a little as the group moved towards her. Escape was impossible because Marjorie blocked her way. They were soon up to her and quite clearly very tiddly.

"Ere, Miss Edgecombe, are you bringing a bloke to the Christmas Party next week?"

Eloise stepped up and glared at the girl who asked the question who backed off quickly. But before she could say something supportive, Ruth uncharacteristically spluttered, "Yes, actually, I am."

They all gawped at her.

"He's a nice chap, I er met him, at er..."

One of the girls turned to her friend and said, "She don't sound too sure!"

Eloise whispered in the girl's ear, "Hush your mout' girl, now!"

Ruth spluttered and realised that the champagne was to blame, "...the gymnasium, he's a swimming partner. Nice man. Ex army. You'll like him for sure. He might just be busy though. Anyway, that's enough of that, how about more champagne?"

She waved three fingers at the bar tender, who nodded and took her bank card from a jar on the shelf to make the payment.

The girls cheered, forgot all about their question and deserted her for the bar; that ended the inquisition.

Just as she was beginning to remonstrate with herself for being so stupid, something else occurred. The person she disliked most of all in the whole universe was coming towards her. Alice Worthington the Director of Finance and lifelong member of a unique club of one member called 'Bitch of the Year,' loomed into view. Ruth looked at her watch. It was after seven p.m. She concluded that this was obviously the wart hog's watering hole. Time to go.

Too late!

Alice Worthington stood squarely in front of her and purred at her in a pseudo-Kensington accent. "Well, well, Ruthie, you dark horse. I just overheard the juniors at the bar and they were saying that you have a man hidden away!"

Alice was aware that the girls regarded her as the doyen of chic in the company and ensured that she never let them down, in dress or manner. Her slinky beige suit, with a shimmering white blouse underneath, always unbuttoned to the point of indecency looked fantastic. Only her make-up betrayed the long day that she had worked, as the powdered surface gave way to the sundry pressures of crow's feet and laughter lines. Instinctively, she reached out, flicked a speck off Ruth's shoulder and sniffed.

"I have too many dear, that's my problem. Then I get fed up and dump them."

Ruth flushed. "Actually I..."

Alice interrupted. "Oh don't give me any soft soap. I have to get home to touch up the paint-work and meet my new man," she paused for effect. "I must tell absolutely everyone to be ready to meet your Mr Right at the party."

She swirled around, looking over her shoulder laughing as she did so.

Ruth tried to call after her, to explain that he was no such thing, but her voice trailed off, sentences unfinished.

"Damn," she thought, "damn, damn, damn!"

She stood, face like thunder and shaking with rage.

"Why did I let myself in for this?"

After about ten minutes she pulled herself together. Then she felt a tap on her shoulder. It was Eloise who was holding a glass of champagne.

"Here we go Miss Edgecombe. You's gonna need this!" she said, with a knowing look on her face.

Ruth took the glass. Eloise always called everyone 'girl', even her, but now she was Miss Edgecombe. Her eyes were soft now, not feisty, and she seemed strangely respectful.

"Dat chick, Worthington, is sometin' ain't she?"

Ruth smiled and sipped her champagne. "You could say that."

Eloise continued, looking straight at her. "You gonna t'ink me a bitch too, but I quite like you."

Ruth waited for the other shoe to drop.

"You don't have a feller do you?"

Ruth put her glass down a little more heavily than she intended. She shared her life with no one. She confided in no one.

"Eloise, I know you mean well, but I do have a chap. He is a little shy and just a friend, but he does exist. Thank you for your support, I really do appreciate it. Oh and by the way, I wanted to thank you for your excellent work on the cover for the Franks project. Good work. Must dash."

The sudden switch to the topic was smooth, but didn't fool Eloise, who gently but firmly took her arm.

"T'anks, you're a nice lady," then she thrust a card into her hand. "I am doin' my Christmas shoppin' tomorrow so won't be in, but I will finish my part of the marketing project. You bet I will. Bye now."

Then she was gone. Ruth had no time to say anything or to ask what Eloise was doing.

She looked at the card, which had embossed lettering in tasteful gold letters. It read: Casey's **Escort Agency – confidential and**

**sensitive to your entire escort needs!** There was a telephone number. Ruth fumed gently and stuffed it into her pocket.

Back in her apartment she took a call from her mother reminding her of the upcoming family party which was always held the Sunday prior to Christmas. It was only the weekend after next. It was getting too close and she had to make arrangements. On top of all that, she had to sort out a more immediate challenge: the office party next week.

She was aware that it was now a problem of her own making.

The next day the workload was surprisingly light. After a few short meetings she had some letters to write and did so quickly and efficiently. She was pleased to hear from the office manager that the Franks' project was proceeding to schedule and some congratulations were in order for the motivational one hour off the day before. It had been a good investment, galvanising the office teams, much to the surprise of the manager. The staff used their lunch-hour to put up some decorations in line with company policy that this could be done only ten days before the annual holiday.

But today, there was an air of merriment about and a feeling of mischievousness pervaded the air. Then it came to her. Alice Worthington had obviously done her worst and that was probably the explanation as to why, every so often, she saw groups of girls turning and looking at her office window. Some giggled. It annoyed her, but she was tough enough to take it. It was a good time to take an early exit home and she grabbed her coat to put it on. As she put her hand in her pocket she noticed the business card. It was the one the one Eloise had given her and she sat down again, put it on the table and leaned back in her chair. She felt intimidated by this small piece of card and it might as well have been as big as a paving stone, it had such presence.

She got up and went to the window and looked out on the broad view of the river Thames and the city which always calmed her and helped her to think. There was a light knock at the door and one of the juniors came in with a cup of coffee. Surprised, Ruth realised the business card was face up on the table and almost shouted at her.

"Over here, the coffee, I'll take it by the window – thank you."

The junior nearly spilled it and was glad to leave.

Ruth took the coffee and sat down. Reluctantly, she reached for the business card and read the telephone number. She was a realist, after all, who would know. Resigned to her fate, it would cost little pride to fix up an escort to get her out of her predicament. She reached for the telephone and dialled. It would of course be on her terms and very temporary. And only someone that was, well, acceptable. Not a smoker, definitely not. Memories of unsuccessful internet dating some years ago flooded back, where specifications for tall men ended up with five foot five inch silver haired strangers, and outward going was interpreted as a liking for hill walking.

"No more of that please," she thought.

A camp American voice answered. "Hello, Casey's Escort Agency, how can I he'p you?"

"Er, hello. I need an escort," she blurted through a dry mouth, "for, um, a party next Wednesday."

"Well, hon', you've come to the right place, Miss, Mrs...?"

"Edgecombe, Ruth Edgecombe, and it's Miss."

"Age and other details please?" said the voice.

Ruth felt as though she was undergoing an embarrassing medical examination. She gave her age, height and build, as well as information about the event that she wanted an escort for and hated every minute of it, gritting her teeth throughout the exchange.

"There must be terms, I mean, behaviour, habits and so on and ..."

The voice interrupted. "Thank you Miss Edgecombe, but my dear, the only terms are payment, the rest you negotiate with the escort. We don't get into all that matching business, this is datin' not social care. Take it or leave it I'm afraid. Okay now?"

She quietly fumed and was angry at having little time to shop around.

The voice continued, "Two hundred and fifty pounds per date."

"Er, um, ..." Ruth spluttered.

"Supply and demand dear, we only have one left. It's the time of year y'know," said the voice without sympathy.

"Oh sod it, okay, okay!"

Ruth gave her credit card number and in return received a name and telephone number of the escort.

The voice added a caution.

"Now listen carefully, ma'am. On no account do you give your own telephone number to the escort. A mobile number perhaps, but not your home number, or your address for that matter. All our escorts are vetted, but you can't ever be too careful. Do you understand that?"

"Okay," said Ruth almost imitating the camp American urban nasal drawl, then he hung up.

She stared at her notepad for a long while and then folded the paper up and put it in her handbag.

The next day passed quickly enough and Ruth remembered that she hadn't confirmed to her mother that she was able to be at the family lunch prior to Christmas. She wanted to buy a couple of bottles of her mother's favourite desert wine, Barsac, and so decided to leave the office early. Ruth put on her Russian style coat with the large fur collar and cuffs and walked through the office wishing everyone a good weekend. Unfortunately, there were still the nods and knowing looks, how she could have kicked herself!

She reached the reception desk on the ground floor, her heels clicked loudly as she crossed the marble tiles, and she waved at the ladies at the desk. One of them looked surprised.

"Oh, Miss Edgecombe, I am sorry. I thought you was in work, crikey Moses, I only just put your mum through to your extension," said the receptionist. "I hope that was okay?"

Ruth thought for a moment and said, "Oh that's a shame my number will be on voice mail."

The receptionist smiled broadly. "Oh I know, so I put her through to your assistant, you know, young Sue – she'll take a message for you."

Ruth blanched and closed her eyes. She was alert enough to see the problem. Sue, was the girl that could deliver a whole year's gossip to one person in five minutes flat. Her mind flashed through the possibilities in a nanosecond

The office party – a partner.

"Good grief," she thought to herself, "tell me this is not happening?"

She thanked the receptionist and rushed outside the office block, looking up to the second floor where her department was located. At first she saw nothing and some relief momentarily flowed, before her hopes were dashed. Sue came into view with a phone held to her ear and was talking at great length into it.

She then turned and waved, pointing to the 'phone.

Ruth smiled weakly and waved to her. It was difficult to remain calm. Perhaps Sue was just chatting about the weather – there was no need to be hasty.

Saturday was spent buying Christmas presents and relaxing, as best she could. Her nerves felt shredded; work pressure she could deal with but all this rubbish was painfully irritating. She had to drum up the courage to phone the escort, but kept putting it off.

The next day, Sunday, Ruth called in to see her mother, to drop Christmas presents off and to confirm her attendance the following weekend. Her Audi TT sports convertible had hardly come to a halt when the front door to the house was flung open and her mother almost burst out of it, arms open wide.

"Darling, how nice to see you, I thought you might be too busy. Oh and is that my favourite wine I see, you are a dear?"

Ruth's father came out of the study, which was close to the front door and smiled broadly. Why? He usually contained his excitement at seeing his daughters, by pretending to be busy, then looking up feigning surprise. Something was afoot.

"Pumpkin," he shouted and hugged her.

Ruth winced - pumpkin? Something was up.

For about an hour they made lots of small talk and exchanged news. Her sister, husband and children could make the pre-Christmas lunch. It was a quaint family habit that neither daughter ever thought of saying they couldn't make it and each year discussion was as though Christmas festivities were being arranged for the first time. Such are family traditions, a cross between a regimental parade and an optional church service. Ruth ran through past reasons she and her sister had been given for obligatory attendance. The first Christmas bash after the birth of a grandchild, to celebrate a new promotion, after an illness, the guinea pig's pregnancy, and so on, there was always a good reason. Neither daughter objected and neither wanted to blink first.

For all that, she loved her parents and never wanted to let them down. Later in the day, her father kept asking her about her business deals. He was genuinely interested and hated being retired even though it had now been at least five years since he left his job in insurance. He sat in thrall when she described various tricky negotiations with clients and, without him being aware that the problems had long since been solved, she adroitly sought his advice, which he duly gave. Ruth always felt good doing this. She knew that it helped him regain a little prestige, thinking that he had some experience to offer.

Mother exchanged family gossip. But, today something was definitely up. Her parents were sitting very close and both had their hands on their knees, whilst leaning towards each other looking a bit like a human 'gothic arch'.

Then the boil popped

"Darling, we are so pleased," said her mother blurted, with a benign smile. "Why didn't you tell us?"

Ruth's mind worked overtime and then the lights went on! Sue - the 'phone call, the office party.

Without waiting for a reply and on cue, her mother continued. "The young man. The gymnasium. The office party. Your lovely staff told me and they are very excited for you, and very pleased."

Then she looked up doe-eyed at Ruth's father. "We are, aren't we Pops?"

"Mum, it's really just..." but she didn't get to finish and her mother continued excitedly.

"That's it settled dear. He must come to pre-Christmas lunch next week, he really must. If he's good enough for the office party then he's good enough for us. I have to tell you darling, I am so excited for you!"

There was such persuasive force that even Ruth, with all her negotiating and board room experience, found it difficult to find the right words to get out of the situation. The best she could offer failed completely.

"But, mum, it's such short notice for you, and ..." she blurted.

"Nonsense," both parents said in unison with the unbridled enthusiasm of a vagrant diving after a five-pound note blowing past in the wind.

"We can always make room for one more. That's settled then. I'll phone your sister right now," said her mother, who virtually bounced out of the living room and into the hallway leaving absolutely no chance for Ruth to disagree.

Her father continued the interrogation. "What's his name?"

Ruth was in shock and tried to keep her wits about her. She had written the escort's name down along with all his other details, but had momentarily forgotten. "Name, ah yes, right well it's …" then her brain engaged first gear and she said quickly, "Sean. That's it, Sean. Nice name eh?"

"Sean, what, dear?" he said.

Ruth decided that this was time to stop.

"Okay, Pops, no more interrogation. Let's talk about something else eh?"

Her father looked perplexed, but decided to stick with the fact that she was bringing a feller to lunch and that was reward enough!

The smell of a roast lunch pervaded the room as her mother opened the kitchen door having made her telephone call to her second daughter. The wonderful aroma had almost magical powers, to quell family arguments, relieve stress, engender a feeling of security, or to create an environment for discussion or relaxation. For Ruth it was a cue to think fast.

The day ended peacefully with mother and father smiling like Cheshire cats at almost every opportunity. Ruth managed to leave without any further questions. On her way home, her heart pumping with fury and anxiety, she decided that she had to phone the escort as soon as she got back to the flat – it was beginning to look as though he would have a double date.

Ruth stood in her study, phone in hand and listened to a voice say, "Hello?" It had a distinctly attractive Irish tang to it.

"Sean Donnelly here."

Ruth was taken aback for a second. What had she expected, a character from East-Enders or Coronation Street?

"Oh, er, hello, um," she mumbled, feeling like a little girl on her first date. "I believe that you are assigned to me, Ruth Edgecombe?"

"Assigned? What is this now, am I on a secret mission to Russia or do you want me to infiltrate the London Stock Exchange?"

She didn't know whether or not to laugh or continue.

"Oh, right, look I'm sorry it's been one of those days. Let's start again."

"Pity," he said, "I thought my luck had changed and was rather looking forward to something exciting. Well there you go now, what's it to be then?"

He was infectiously cheerful, so much so that she was beginning to feel quite good about the situation. There was something about him already, amusing, entertaining, and magnetic almost. Ruth was beginning to like him, but all the same, said guardedly, "Smolenskey's on the Strand. Jazz restaurant. Office party a week on Wednesday. Usual stuff. But I want to meet you and brief you first."

"Ah! Then I'm your man. I understand the situation too. You want to see if I'm balding, spectacled and have cross eyes, eh?" He laughed loudly.

She regained the upper hand, but had to repress the urge to laugh.

"Not at all. In fact if you were like that you'd probably fit in very well indeed. No, I just want things to go well and for there to be no misunderstandings. Are you all right with that? We can meet for a drink or two, my shout!"

He responded cheerily. "Yes ma'am. If I was paying the going rate for an escort I would want to check out the goods too, so I promise to wear a clean vest and brush my teeth. But I think I can manage to pay my way too y'know, let's keep this as, say, a business visit?"

He continued without waiting for a reply. "Only don't make it before eight p.m. I have to visit my aged bed-ridden aunt, go to communion then give some Red Cross collection boxes back to the organiser."

"Gosh. Really?"

There was a pause.

"No, not at all, but for a second you almost liked me so much that you could've put off the inspection!" He laughed again and Ruth was not very amused, she didn't like being wrong-footed.

"This man is bloody-well teasing me," she thought to herself. "I'll have to match his wit."

She waited and continued. "Let's say, the Sherlock Holmes public house tomorrow night, it's on Northumberland Avenue, do you know it?"

"Ah yes, I know that pub very well. Elementary, my dear Miss Edgecombe, elementary!"

His wit was now so obvious she was almost expecting that response. Without further ado she ended the conversation and put the telephone down.

What had she done?

As she approached the Sherlock Holmes public house the following night, Ruth felt her feet get heavier and heavier with every step along the damp pavement. She was normally in control of herself, but in this situation she felt out of her depth, or at least out of control and she didn't like that one bit. The large wooden door swung behind her as she entered the pub. Looking around the bar for a man standing on his own, one man stood out. He was blonde, had a medium build with a good body and dishy smile, immaculately dressed in a beige linen suit with a pink shirt. He glanced up and shot her a ready smile. But as she walked slowly over to where he was standing, he turned away. Halfway to the bar she felt a tap on her shoulder. Ruth wheeled around and was confronted by a man with short dark hair wearing jeans and a roll neck beige sweater. He was quite tall, slim and had big green eyes, a square jaw and a broad cheeky dimpled grin. She couldn't help but glance back at the blonde man at the bar.

"Ah, so that's it. You thought Mr Robert Redford over there was Sean Donnelly."

His shoulders drooped theatrically and he pulled such a funny face she burst out laughing.

"No, why, I was just looking for a man alone, and ..."

"Jeez, looking for a man alone, you're my kind of woman!" he said as he pretended to spring back into life.

"But do not worry, Miss Ruth Edgecombe, you've hit the jackpot!"

He pointed his hands at his chest, then slowly leaned forward and whispered conspiratorially, nodding toward the fair-haired man at the bar, "Anyways, he's gay you know? Lovely feller, but such a disappointment to his old mum."

"Gosh, why you'd never..." she blurted.

He laughed spontaneously and she knew she'd been had again. How did this guy do it?

Taking her arm, he led her to a table. She hated being led.

Ruth calmed herself and accepted a gin and tonic and he brought himself a large Guinness.

"Here's your gin, I would've guessed that gin or Chardonnay is your tipple."

"Well, you would've been correct," she said. "Now let's get down to business."

In fact they did anything but get down to business. He effortlessly controlled the discussion as though he were a professional conversationalist. They talked about life, work, siblings and their favourite city, London. Her hard attitude to a blind date began to soften.

He was not a stunning man, but he was good looking. His quick wit and ready smile made him an amusing date. Ruth knew enough about men to know that men who succeeded in breaching the 'St Michael' elastic line were those who made women laugh. She knew that much and guarded against it.

Sean swallowed his second Guinness and put the glass down heavily. "Okay then, Ruth, do I pass?"

She waited before answering and decided to take a serious line, despite the fact that they had got on so well.

"Yes you do Sean, but I promise that was not what this was all about. Now let's turn to the script," and she handed him some notes. "I want you to learn our cover story."

Sean's eyebrows shot upwards. "Cover story?"

Ruth continued. "My work colleagues have interrogation skills that wouldn't have been out of place in the Kremlin. Oh, for the record, we met at a local gymnasium and swim, and that sort of thing. We have shared interests such as, fitness, theatre, literature and ballet..."

Sean spluttered. "Ballet...?"

"Oh okay, forget the ballet," she said with some reservation. "I suppose I can't have everything?"

He held the notes at arm's length and looked alarmed as he read it aloud. "Theatre, literature, ballet, Jesus Mary, who are you looking to date, Andrew bloody Lloyd-Webber? Or am I to be the male version of Pygmalion?"

Ruth's face softened. It was time to go.

"Sean, look, that's the deal. Take it or leave it, eight p.m. on Wednesday at this pub, dress is jacket and tie – smart of course - then we will take a taxi to Smolensky's," she placed a finger on his nose, "and for good measure, Mr Donnelly, there is another duty next Sunday. It's for lunch with my parents, same script, same price and here's the address. We'll go in your car. I take it you own one?"

He blanched, confirmed that he was mobile and he would be on parade booted and spurred to meet the times in her brief. Then he stood to attention and saluted, wearing a big grin from ear to ear. She wanted to laugh some more, but somehow, just somehow, this was a desperately serious issue for her and she just wanted him to play his part and play it well – then push off.

She stood up and grabbed her coat.

"Don't be late, or I'll take a contract out on you!" she said over her shoulder as she was leaving.

He wasn't God's gift to women, but he was very amusing company and she hadn't laughed so much in a man's company for a long time.

Outside, the cold breeze hit her face and chilled her. It brought her down to earth. This may be amusing, but it was certainly not going to be easy, she knew that much.

Roll on the New Year!

Wednesday morning was nothing short of a nightmare. Two key accounts had to have their targets revised to meet the clients' demands. The usual excuse: can they finish the job before the New Year? It never seemed to dawn on them to ask this in November rather than late December. Nevertheless, her best staff managed to meet the challenge despite the excitement of the approaching office party, whilst the juniors kept peeking into bags marked, M & S, Next or Debenhams and squealing. Others sipped more than they should of the mulled wine that the MD had warmed up himself that morning. Trying to keep them focused was a Herculean task.

Very soon Ruth was aware that her biggest challenge was going to be the office gossips. In this respect age knows no barrier and Ruth's department had a secret society all of its own, and were well trained practitioners with A1 qualifications. They rather advertised their latest interest and it was Ruth, by frequently looking at her office and tilting their heads to talk to their colleagues at the same time. Short of 'outing' herself as a lesbian, she couldn't have attracted more interest.

She reflected on her stupidity and to her surprise, found herself wishing that Sean Donnelly was drop dead gorgeous, just to teach them all a lesson. Then she chastised herself, he wasn't bad looking at all. Besides, one couldn't own everything that was perfect in life – she certainly was not. If she was honest, she had let many a good man pass because they had not been able to 'pop her toast'.

Shaking her head she got back to work. The day continued without crisis and before she knew it, it was four forty-five p.m. and time to leave. On her way out she reminded staff to be at Smolensky's on time. There would be no speeches, just lots of good food, cocktails and jazz. Then her tummy froze a little, oh and of course, the floorshow: Ruth and her supposed new man.

Ruth closed her eyes and dreamed of Christmas Day, by which time it would all be over: the office party and the family pre-Christmas lunch. But for now it was home to bathe, make up and dress in something black and slinky, a couple of stiff gins and off to the Sherlock Holmes pub to collect her escort.

Reflecting, Ruth felt quite pleased at manoeuvring her way out of a problem. Now it was actually two problems, but that did not matter. It would soon pass. She had half-written the script already. Family and friends would be told that although she and Sean had enjoyed each other's company, and their relationship might have even blossomed, each had too many pressures to cope with. They parted good friends and agreed to stay in touch. Yes that was it, just good friends. To ensure a proper closure she would tell them that he had to go to, Argentina or perhaps New Guinea. Both places were far enough away from the UK to prevent comment. She would, of course, give him some credit and say that he was building a convent, or an orphanage. That would close the loop and her life could return to normal.

Ruth was smiling to herself when she walked into the Sherlock Holmes public house. Her smile soon disappeared.

Leaning against the bar, trying to get his lips to engage with a glass of Guinness was Sean. Although smartly dressed, his cream shirt and tie sported a large red stain. She assessed the situation quickly.

He had either been shot in the chest fairly recently or failed to negotiate a large hot dog full of tomato sauce. She opted for the tomato assessment. A large pot-bellied man with a T-shirt that advertised, *'Dave's Dogs,'* stood next to him laughing and pointing at Sean, who was heard saying, "Oh no!"

Ruth was not amused and strode up to him.

"Sean, what's going on?"

She noticed his glazed look. He wasn't drunk, but he was well on the way. The situation looked precarious. It was not possible for him to go to the office party in his current state. Ruth gazed at the ceiling and considered the options open to her. What could she say if he didn't turn up? He was wanted for murder; had to go to 10 Downing Street for a security briefing, or perhaps more plausibly, he had double pneumonia? The pneumonia sounded good and for two hoots she would tip him into the street to help it develop, then explain to her colleagues that he was in hospital.

The trouble was that no one would believe her. So it was onwards and upwards. She reached out and took Sean by the scruff of the neck and looked inside his collar. It was labelled fifteen and half inches. Turning towards his bar-stool friend, the hot-dog musketeer, she barked. "You, yes you," and she reached into her bag and took out a fifty pound note, handing it to him. "He has to be at a function in a short while. It is important. Go to a men's shop, there's one a hundred yards to the right towards Trafalgar Square that's open late for Christmas shoppers. Get him a new shirt and tie, please be sure to make sure they match, and nothing gopping! Oh, and it must be non-iron shirt. Well what are you waiting for?"

The man looked surprised at first, then the realisation that he was responsible and had to make amends hit him, and he quickly exited the public house on a mission to get a shirt. Ruth hoped he would come back. The rest of the clientele, though few in number, looked on approvingly and the bar staff tried to conceal their smiles. This made good entertainment.

Sean tried to order another Guinness, but Ruth put up her hand to the bar tender. "Coffee, please, several of them, black and strong. Thank you so much."

The barman nodded and turned to go to the kitchen. Sean turned to Ruth, looked guilty and winced.

"Sorry, darlin' I..."

Ruth broke in. "Sean, you have nothing to say that would even interest me in any way at all. And don't call me darling. Now get sober and let's get you ready to escort me to Smolensky's as we agreed. You owe me that much!"

Furious, she walked outside and took some air. It was cold, but she didn't mind, it cooled her flushed face and made her feel better.

Sean consumed six small cups of strong black coffee, much to the amusement of the waitress and sobered up quite quickly. Just as he finished the last coffee, 'Dave the Dog-man,' returned with the shirt and tie, and obediently showed them to Ruth. They were a good match, light blue shirt and a navy check tie. He held out the change from the fifty pounds and she pointed to the RNIB charity box on the counter.

Twenty minutes later Sean sheepishly stood in front of her as a taxi drew up. He looked smart and surprisingly sober and that was enough for her. Sean turned to her and started to say something, but she just turned and got into the waiting vehicle. Smolensky's jazz restaurant is not far from the Sherlock Holmes public house, but Ruth wanted to arrive without looking wind-swept.

They travelled in silence.

As they got out of the taxi and Ruth was paying the fare, several office juniors wearing party hats came up to her blowing their part trumpets and waving tinsel. They gawped at Sean. Ruth was about to say something when Sean burst into life.

"My goodness, what's this, do all these beautiful women work with you?" he said his lilting Irish accent, oozing with charm.

The girls cooed and laughed.

Ruth forced a crooked smile and said guardedly, "Sean, you are a charmer if ever there was one!"

They all moved down the steps into Smolensky's and as they did so Sean was laughing and baiting the girls who clearly loved every minute of it. He moved to the bar to get them both drinks.

The music was loud and the main bar to the right of the restaurant was packed with partygoers. It was just what Ruth wanted, relative safety in numbers. But this was not to be the case. Her stomach churned when she looked up. Alice Worthington was headed straight for Ruth and Sean, eyebrows raised and a wicked smile on her face. Then surprisingly, Alice stopped in her tracks, smiled meekly and moved off at a tangent, making out she had seen someone else to talk to.

Ruth was surprised, but elated. "Dear Lord, thank you for your small, but oh so important mercies."

She turned and to her disbelief saw Sean propping up the bar, surrounded by several ladies from the office, champagne in hand, quite the bon viveur. He was just finishing a joke at the end of which they burst into laughter, then turned to Ruth and shouted.

"Hey, Ruth, you didn't tell me what good company your colleagues are? I bet you never have a dull moment at work?" he said, smiling from ear to ear. He swigged rather than sipped the champagne and Ruth blanched at every swallow, forcing a smile. How much alcohol could this man take?

"Yes, a laugh a minute!" she said, and waved an arm half-heartedly, at the same time accepting a glass of champagne.

The ladies finally let go of Sean and made their way to the restaurant leaving Sean and Ruth to walk from the bar to the main restaurant together.

"Great party already!" he said. Then, before she could tell him ease back on the champagne her MD's voice boomed out.

"Ruth. Good to see you. Come and join us and bring your chap with you, why don't you?"

He grabbed Sean's hand and introduced himself.

Sean shook his hand and said, "Sean Donnelly. Nice to meet you, sir. I am grateful you let an outsider like me in to join you on this special night."

"No problem. Any friend of Ruth's is a friend of ours."

The MD guided him deftly away from Ruth with his arm on Sean's shoulder, adding, "Quite a catch, dear boy, quite a catch. How did you do it, you must tell me?"

The MD's wife, Gill, held Ruth in conversation for longer than she wanted but eventually she excused herself and caught up with Sean and the MD, just as he was asking how they met. She quickly answered that it was the gymnasium as Sean said the library - so much for her briefing notes. The evening was going from bad to worse.

They made a joke of it and Sean retrieved the situation using his charm and ready wit. By this time he was in his element. They went to an allocated table and all Ruth could do was to impotently let the evening roll – she was out of the control loop. She did not like this one little bit – her life was all about control and this was a nightmare to her.

Sean quipped, joked and fooled around and the MD and guests couldn't stop laughing. As the evening wore on the jokes got spicier. After talking about sport, it was a monologue on politics and the problems with the current government. But when he got to a sentence that started, "...and another thing that bothers me..." she decided it was time to go.

Luckily, it was well after two in the morning and the restaurant had thinned considerably with most of the guests now on their way home.

"Okay, Sean, shall we hit the road?" she said, trying to hide her impatience.

Sean wanted to visit more clubs and see the night away and had the support of the remaining audience, but Ruth persisted, glaring a little too obviously at him. He recognised a lost cause and took the hint, but not before standing shakily on a chair and giving them all a few verses of, "When Irish Eyes Are Smiling", much to their delight and wild applause. Ruth thought she had died and gone to hell.

Once outside and out of sight of the restaurant, Ruth turned to him and let rip.

"Sean, you ignored me, you chatted up all the women, told dirty jokes to my MD and frankly you were boorish. And what's more the false story you made up about you and me caught snogging in the library was just too much."

She fumed and almost stamped her feet.

"Oh," he said, like a little schoolboy, "but apart from that you had a good time, eh?"

"No, I did not, Sean. And I could never have with you, ever. Do you understand," she replied, red in the face. "And forget the lunch on Sunday. I'll get by. I'll tell them you went to the South Pole or something. Just don't turn up. Damn you!"

As hard as she was, Sean thought he saw traces of tears in her eyes. Just then a taxi stopped for her. She reached into her bag and withdrew an envelope, which she pushed into his hand.

"Thank you, Mr Donnelly. Your fee I believe. It's all there, for both tasks in fact. So you made on the deal. I wish you the compliments of the season," she said icily and got in the taxi.

Sean stared at her and then back at the envelope. He wanted to say something, but no sound came.

He watched the taxi drive off into the dimly lit streets.


The next day Ruth sat and ate her breakfast looking out of her large window overlooking Tower Bridge and the River Thames. Her yoghurt tasted foul and only the coffee offered her some comfort. She didn't go for a swim, because it had been too late a night and it was hard enough to get up for work. That put her in a bad mood for a start. After dressing she decided to walk to work to rid herself of her aching head and get some oxygen before having to take the digs she would get at Sean's antics. More humiliation would surely follow and was resigned to it. It was all her stupid fault. She would take it on the chin then move on - it would all blow over.

As she walked into the company reception area Doris the receptionist looked up and said, "Miss Edgecombe, oh that bloke you brought to the party, where did you get him, he is such a card?"

Ruth smiled politely. "Yes, Doris quite a character isn't he?"

She resisted the urge to say, "Oh yeah?"

Several girls looked up as she walked to her office and seemed more jovial than usual. Ruth expected some sarcasm or jokes at her expense, but there were none at all. Eventually, Sue the junior knocked then came into her office.

"Hey, Miss Edgecombe, I 'ope you don't mind me sayin' what a nice feller you have. He's absolutely bril'! Not stuck up and such fun, a real regular feller," then she corrected herself. "Not that we thought you would have chosen anyone stuck-up or toffee-nosed or anyfing."

"Yes," Ruth said, and repeated the mantra, "he's quite a character!"

"Too right. Pity you had to leave. He came back in and joined us at the bar. He made a lot of friends when he dealt with that mouthy little git from the IT department on the fourth floor. Sorry, better out than in. You know the young manager with the spikey hair and loud ties? Anyway, he was touching up young Angela, poor kid she was embarrassed. You know how nice and innocent she is. Your Sean steered him firmly away and challenged him to a yard of ale and guess what, he won! Gawd, Miss, didn't we arf cheer!"

Ruth listened in awe.

"Then, blimey you'll never believe it, I 'ope I'm not talking out of turn, but when Lucy told us she was preggers, he organised a collection for her baby and started it off by putting in two hundred and fifty pounds, yes, two hundred and fifty pounds!"

Ruth looked at the ceiling and wondered what next.

"That's not all eever. Marjorie said that earlier in the evening when he first arrived, she was getting wed and said he knew this geezer who had a Bentley. Anyway, guess what?"

Ruth almost knew some kind of largesse was coming to accompany this last 'guess what'.

"He will fix up for her to have it for her wedding day. What a gent', what a lovely bloke. I just thought I'd say that. We all love him, he's really a goodun, in fact we all say it. Give him a big kiss from us!"

Then as quickly as she came in, she left, having said all she wanted to. Ruth was a dazed and she looked out of the internal office window onto the open plan office floor. To her astonishment, the girls had their heads down and were working like crazy and every now and then one would look up smile and raise a thumb.

Ruth tried to take it all in. She went to the coffee machine on the first floor and got a double espresso. That would wake her up. It was all a dream – yes a dream. Worse was to come, she knew it. As she got back to her office she saw the MD coming.

"Oh, my sainted aunt!" she thought.

Everyone has to go to the MD, he never ever comes to them. By the time he reached her door she had worked out her redundancy package and leaving date. He peered into her office and smiled, almost conspiratorially.

"Ruth, my dear. Just thought that I would pop in and see you!"

"Here it comes," she thought, "Sean's behaviour was unbecoming of an executive's guest, or he vomited on the floor? Touching up his wife or an ice cube in her cleavage was a possibility too. Lack of political correctness perhaps?"

He continued. "That man of yours, what's his name, er…"

"Sean," she replied, hesitantly.

"Yes, Sean. Bloody nice bloke. Bloody nice. Never laughed so much in all my life, is he like that all the time? Ah, but you know that already I bet. Did you know he was an ex-paratrooper. I wanted to join the Parachute Regiment but couldn't, bad back, still never mind. Anyway, his story about parachuting off course and crashing into an open air wedding was a cracker, especially when he said to the vicar, 'If I get there first she's mine!' "

He was obviously considerably amused and went on. "Apparently he was a teacher for a while at an inner London school, but quit because of the paperwork and lack of reality. Gill was a teacher too you know and could relate to that, they got on famously. I just wanted to say what a great laugh he was. Best time I've had for ages - mighty fine company."

He half turned to go, then said, "Jolly good chap, my girl, great to meet him."

Then he was gone. Ruth felt dazed. He was quite a catch?

She looked down - her coffee was cold.

Friday went by quicker than Thursday and the Franks' account was not only finished, but much to everyone's delight it was the very best piece of teamwork they had ever put together. There was a real buzz in the air. It would be delivered with a fanfare to the customer that very day, just before the Christmas break.

Ruth looked at the bottles of champagne that she received as part of her bonus and felt some elation at least, but the events of the last twenty-four hours still clouded her mind. On the one hand, she had avoided the embarrassment of not having a partner at the office party and on the other, she felt sorry that she had sent a perfectly reasonable chap off with a flea in his ear, even if he deserved it. She went home gloomy instead of fired-up from the good work done at the office.

Saturday came and went too. She bought more presents in London and finished the day off at the local spa with a well-deserved bit of pampering. In the spa they played her favourite Nina Simone numbers and she fell asleep in the Jacuzzi only to wake up suddenly, seeing Sean's face appearing out of the bubbles. On focussing more clearly, she saw that it wasn't a face, but a woman's bathing cap bobbing up and down. Why did she call up his image? Perhaps she wanted to drown him, yes, that was it, to drown him.

Sunday brought with it the realisation that her parents would feel disappointed when they learned that the mysterious Sean wouldn't be with them for lunch. They would get over it. But it did make her think that perhaps she could arrange an escort for the Easter lunch. If Sean was going to be good enough today, why not some other chap, perhaps a Robert Redford lookalike, just to please them?

Her Audi TT sports car pulled up outside the family home, the wheels crunching the gravel as it slid to a halt. She sat for a moment listening to an old favourite tune on her CD player, Alison Moyet's, *That ole devil called love*, and gathered her thoughts.

"What's it to be," she thought. "Argentina for Sean perhaps, I'll say that he wants to be a corned beef merchant. He desperately wanted to meet you both, etc, etc. Or, perhaps New Guinea, or a tummy bug perhaps? Maybe something more prosaic, like: we realised we had nothing in common, cried a lot and left each other without a backward glance."

She harrumphed out loud, irritated at having to develop such a script.

The front door to the house opened and her mother appeared.

Gathering her wits she decided to deliver the right excuse at the right time, but not straight away.

"Darling," said her mother, craning her head around the door looking for another form, not seeing anyone else, but not actually asking about Sean, "come in out of the cold, we're all here."

She looked disappointed but to her great credit said nothing.

Her father hurried into the hallway and he too looked slightly disappointed.

"It's building up," thought Ruth.

"Hello, pumpkin," he said and pecked her on the cheek.

Ruth went to the garden room and was greeted by her sister and brother-in-law. Their twin daughters Harriet and Jemima squealed at the sight of her and hugged her knees. She grabbed them and was glad of the diversion before the interrogation that would surely follow. Her mother and father were doing that leaning thing again, looking like badly made bookends.

Thankfully the twins begged to receive their presents and she dutifully did what aunties do and gave in. It bought more time. Moments later her mother came in with six champagne glasses half full – she never overdid anything. Ruth knew she would have to say something very soon and the sixth glass was now a focal point for everyone. It stood there on the silver tray, the 'elephant in the room', almost omnipresent, quietly fizzing and taking on a dimension far greater than its actual size.

When they each had a glass in hand, the sixth sitting on the tray, alone and unloved, her father raised his Champagne and said. "Well now, here's a toast to Christmas, that happy time of year and our lovely family." He turned apologetically to Ruth and looked a little confused. "Darling, I'm sorry we can't wait for Sean, lunch is twenty minutes away. We can keep his food nice and warm if he is delayed for a lot longer."

Everyone was about to drink the health of Christmas and family, and Ruth was preparing to say something about the situation, her mind working overtime.

Then the doorbell rang.

Ruth's mother nearly jumped out of her skin.

"It's him, Sean, oh lovely," she said like an excited young girl and she rushed to the door. Ruth closed her eyes. It was probably the neighbour saying she had run over their cat. She would wait for her to return before delivering a prepared fib.

Ruth's heart almost stopped.

"Hello, Mrs Edgecombe," said an unmistakable Irish voice. "Jeez, I'm so sorry that I'm late. Traffic all over the place and a Sunday too."

Ruth's eyes widened. It was him. What was he playing at?

Her mother came into the lounge first, and said enthusiastically, "Everyone, this is Sean," pausing before adding definitively, "Ruth's man. Here, Sean, have a glass of champagne, it's so good to see you."

Sean was immaculately dressed in a blazer and beige chino trousers and wore a blue check shirt. Only his suede shoes gave away a slight lack of attention to detail. He accepted the champagne then leaned over and gave Ruth a peck on the cheek apologising for his lateness. Ruth was dumbstruck. Then she looked up and saw to her horror the whole family were looking at them both and flushed. Sean came to the rescue.

"Mr Edgecombe, do you know anything about carburettors, I have a Bentley and it is running badly. I hate to admit it but that was also a reason for my lateness," he said.

Her father almost fell over himself going to the window. "Well no, but I would certainly like to see inside the bonnet."

"So would I," echoed Ruth's brother-in-law.

Sean looked at Ruth, "Is that okay, honey?"

Ruth blanched. Honey? Yuck!

"Yes, fine, but don't be long now," and she smiled sweetly. He pecked her cheek again and whispered in her ear, "Don't worry, I did amateur dramatics once and can carry this through for you."

What would she do now?

Mother gave instructions that they were not to be long and when the men were outside cooed with Ruth's sister about how nice Sean seemed.

The men returned and they all tucked into a splendid lunch, the kind her mother was famous for. Ruth and Sean adroitly ducked several questions about how long they had known each other, fibbing and avoiding issues. Sean made up a couple of 'howlers', but they seemed to go unnoticed, so Ruth didn't mind. They were certainly better than his previous attempt, particularly the snog in the library story.

They ate the lunch, her mother twittered and the twins kept nudging each other as well as Sean, who tickled them several times. It was actually working out very well.

Then during coffee after the meal they talked about work and Sean appeared a little glassy eyed.

"Mr Edgecombe, sorry Jack, Ruth is very clever you know and successful. You must be so proud of her, I know I am," he said.

Ruth stiffened at this compliment which she thought an invasion of her privacy. Her father responded. "Yes we are, aren't we, Mary?"

After a few more minutes of general chitchat, the men went out for some fresh air, Ruth's brother-in-law to sort out some items in the car and Sean and Jack walked to the bottom of the garden.

They stood by the greenhouse, well away from the house and Ruth's father turned to Sean.

"Sean, it is so good to see Ruth with someone like you, I have to say old chap, that I like you already."

"That's nice of you to say that, Jack, but remember we are just good friends, don't expect wedding bells."

"Oh, I know, of course, it's just that she once lost her heart to a young tyke, many years ago and I mean big time. He was much younger than her, but won her round by using all the right language, the bastard swallowed the manual on charm I can tell you. She fell for his soft soap and compliments, and then he just dumped her out of the blue. Well, it really hit her hard. I think it was because she had let her guard down. Ever since then she has been as impenetrable as concrete. Just thought I'd fill you in, okay?"

Sean now understood more about Ruth.

"Jack, rest assured I will never ever treat her badly, you have my word on that."

They returned to the house and Ruth was obviously enduring her mother's non-stop chatter about Sean's charm. For her part Ruth was reasonably happy about Sean's surprise visit, but she worried about his motive. Was he stalking her? This could be difficult and she knew that at the end of this charade she would have to be firm and final – just in case.

Moving to the garden room they walked close together and she became aware of his warm body. She didn't want to admit it, but it felt nice to be close to a man, smelling his warmth and odour and, although an artificial situation, being with someone. Then something inside her made her stiffen and resent the situation.

Sean played with the twins for a while and to their great delight he went out to his coat and brought back two small boxes. They each had a necklace. For the next hour he was Mr Popular. Ruth's mother and father were smitten.

The children left the room and when they were finally alone he said, "My goodness, I had forgotten how much hard work it is to look after two children."

He patted the seat, looking at Ruth as if to encourage her to sit beside him. She obliged, reluctantly and only for form's sake. Her mother popped her head around the door.

"Tea, anyone?"

Sean grabbed Ruth and pulled her onto his lap and she squealed in protest.

"Sorry about your wayward daughter, Mary, yes please, milk no sugar for me."

Ruth fumed inwardly. Mother put her hand to her lips and beamed.

"I don't mind at all, Sean, I'll leave you two love-birds alone for a while," she said. Then she left as quickly as she came in.

Ruth stood up and turned to Sean. "Sean, outside, now!"

Sean looked skywards and rolled his eyes, he knew his sense of humour was an acquired taste but had always found it difficult to take any objection to it seriously. It was now obvious that an execution was coming.

He said loudly, "Oh dear, here we go, red hot irons, bamboo under the fingernails or is it water torture or a tongue lashing at a thousand decibels?"

He followed her gingerly outside.

Ruth harrumphed and marched to the bottom of the garden. Sean hunched his shoulders against the cold, he knew that Ruth needed cooling even if he didn't. He stopped beside her and gazed into her face giving her a wry smile. She stood arms folded and looked skyward.

Then she let loose.

"Sean, why are you here?" she said. "I specifically said the job was off. Are you stalking me, is that it? Do you want more money? Perhaps you get off on this kind of thing, winding women up? Do you realise my poor parents probably have me married off and expecting triplets? Wayward daughter my arse, that was a cheap jibe too. My God," she paused, "the girls. Sean if you ever..."

Sean's face suddenly clouded and he glowered at her. After a short pause he said quietly and firmly, but with a slightly shaky voice, "That's enough. Don't ever imply that again, do you hear me?"

She noticed his fists balled in his pockets.

He went on. "Now you listen to me, Ruth. Don't let your bloody self-importance get the better of you. Use your eyes and your senses girl. You don't understand my situation."

"And what precisely is that?" she questioned.

"Look I goofed. I behaved badly on Wednesday I know that, but I hope I made up for it later?"

"You did goof, you bloody did," she threw at him.

He paused and looked up. "You really don't understand Ruth. It was a bad day. It's always a bad day, on that day, every year. It was the anniversary of my wife's death, she and my two boys were killed in a car crash. It was a drink-driver."

Ruth gasped and was taken aback, but Sean was still angry.

"So I couldn't harm two little girls. Besides, I would never demean my late family's memory by chasing a bit of skirt like you," he said angrily. He folded his arms and turned his back on her.

She gasped at the insult and fumed.

After a few minutes of silence, Sean turned to her and continued more calmly. "But then I guess I know women well enough to know that you're mad and upset and I hope you didn't really mean what you said. But I have to say that you do have a habit of drastically overstating anything that offends your sense of pride or sensibilities."

His eyes were now quite glazed and Ruth, who was by now calmer, realised that it was all getting out of control.

"Sean. Oh goodness, I didn't…well…I'm so dreadfully sorry, but you, here, and …"

"Ah," Sean responded, detecting an insult, "me, here, you mean, 'Mr I'm not quite up to your fine standard of behaviour, Donnelly', eh? Not quite the Sean Bean type? A little thin on top perhaps? Well for your information Miss Arsey Tarsey, your eyebrows are a bit thick and your arse needs to lose a few pounds. Pah!"

Ruth spluttered, "Argh!"

They both stood back to back again.

Sean broke the silence, shrugging his shoulders. "Ruth, this is silly. Look I know I let you down on Wednesday, but as I said, there were special circumstances. If you relaxed a bit, removed your head from your bum and took some time to talk to me you'd understand too. You would also have seen me doing my best to make up for it later in the evening. We all make mistakes, but it's what we do to put things right that matters."

More silence followed.

"Then you sacked me! I've never been bloody sacked in my life!" He went on, "Anyway, I thought I knew how much today meant to you. I wanted to help to out of an awkward situation, you see I did read the brief, and was determined to make it up to you. I just wanted this to be a kind of 'showcase' for you, an excuse for a partner I suppose, then to say farewell, that's all."

He paused and after a while added, "I can't imagine what excuse you would have given to your adoring parents without my presence here today. I only hope that you wouldn't have said that I was banged up for child molestation!"

He stared at her and she looked back at him, her face pale.

"Sean, that's not fair I didn't mean it, really, I'm sorry, I just got mad."

He turned and faced squarely her. "Okay, I understand, and I guess that was a cheap point for me to score. You know, I used to resent the female ability to be sharp when upset, and yes even my loving wife did it sometimes. But, my God, I miss it now, all the time."

He gazed over her shoulder and into the distance.

"For the last time, I really wanted to make up for Wednesday and ensure you kept face with your family. That's all. I'm not as dishonest as your young boyfriend of ten years ago – all men are not the same Ruth."

Ruth was startled.

"Who told you that?"

"Oh, hell. Never mind that. There you go again, offended at the message rather than the meaning. It was your Dad. He was only looking out for you. They may laud you as the successful business woman, Miss feisty and hard as nails, but they want to protect you too you know. Love means a lot of things, Ruth, I don't think you really appreciate what you've got."

Sean looked at his feet and put his collar up, then straightened.

"I'll be gone in twenty minutes. Let's be civilised eh? At least for your parents' sake, then you can let them down gently a bit later. I'm off to spend Christmas in my cottage in Devon so don't worry I won't be hanging around outside your bedroom window."

Then, he smiled broadly and his eyes sparkled with defiance as he added, "nice though that may be".

Arguing can be wearisome and they had both had enough.

Ruth's face softened just a little and she almost half-smiled back.

"And for what it's worth, your eyebrows are lovely and your arse puts Jennifer Lopez's into second place by miles," he raised his head and looked down his nose at her like a fatherly school-teacher.

Before she could answer, he added, "Look, don't get embarrassed about using escorts. Everyone does it. Why I even recognised several of my customers at your office party, Alice Worthington for one. She regularly uses escorts from Casey's, they reckon she has shares in the place."

Ruth's eyes opened wide and she said softly, "Alice...do you know her?"

"Know her? She was one of my first assignments. I spent most of the evening trying to keep her out of my jeans. That bloody woman has an insatiable appetite and it's not for pie and chips."

Ruth imagined Sean fighting off Alice's amorous advances. She was about to try and make amends when he turned towards the house, saying, "Anyway, I gotta go. Nature calls, then," he looked at his watch as he strode away, "off to Devon."

Without waiting for a response he walked directly to the French windows.

Ruth stood silent, thinking about what he had said. She felt desperately stupid. However successful she was at work, her private life was a mess and she knew it. Sean was right, she didn't take time to understand her parents, and other people, often jumping to conclusions and making a meal out of small things. Manipulating people, controlling and influencing them if you want, is all very well, but it has its drawbacks. She didn't take time to listen and understand them. It also didn't need four bottles of 'humanity' pills to see Sean for what he was – a pretty decent man.

She breathed deeply, dabbed her eyes, and came to a conclusion. It was time to do what she was good at: to face up to a problem situation and deal with it. No plans, not too much thinking, no more scripts, but a bit of spontaneity perhaps?

Ruth put her shoulders back and walked purposefully towards the house. As she entered the hallway she heard Sean talking to her parents. The twins were shouting, "Oh no, don't go."

Sean had a kind of resigned look on his face and glanced at her as she came closer.

"Mary, Jack, thank you so much for such a lovely time, one of the best lunches I have had for many a day. You really are such a special family I feel very privileged indeed," he paused slightly to clear his throat, "the fact is..."

This time it was Ruth's turn to interject.

"The fact is, Mummy and Daddy, that Sean and I want to go to his cottage in Devon and spend some time together."

Sean's jaw dropped. Her parents' eyes widened. The rest of the group including the children turned towards Ruth like sunflowers following the light of the sun. Unaffected by the surprised stares she went on.

"Sean and I have been under a lot of pressure at work and well," she gazed at Sean, "well, frankly, we also just want to get to know each other a bit more, on our own. So, there you go, we're off to Devon for Christmas."

Her parents simultaneously clasped their hands in prayer-like fashion and did their 'book-end' impersonation. But she didn't notice and was looking straight at Sean. She saw a different man. He saw a different woman. Without hesitation, she moved closer and pecked his cheek, gently whispering, "I've done a bit of amateur dramatics too you know. Don't get too frisky, Robert Redford, it will be separate rooms and one more comment about my arse and you're dead!"

Her parents stood, almost breathless, watching the exchange, but not hearing the words, their faces a picture of tranquillity. Cupid had at last fallen out of the love tree and hit every branch on the way down - what joy.

Eloise Sobers and her family were preparing themselves for a Caribbean New Year and the air was rich with cheerful voices, joking, singing and lots of loud music. There was a knock at the door, she opened it and saw a delivery man standing on the step.

"Miss Eloise Sobers? This is for you, sign here please?"

The man was clearly eager to get home to his own celebrations.

Eloise looked at the item in his hand. It was a magnum of champagne. She signed for it, lifting the bottle carefully onto the hall table. There was a card attached and when she looked more closely she saw that it was the escort agency business card she had given Ruth Edgecombe.

Across the face of it was a big red tick!

Then her face wreathed in smiles and she said out loud, "Hey girl, you done good, real good – Happy New Year."

# THE PATH TO RANDWYJK

Alexandra Van Der Klerk sat upright against several flimsy cushions and looked out of a smudged window, at a tall, handsome young man with a mass of dark hair and a tanned complexion, and smiled. She knew his name was Jonathon. A few decades ago, well, more than a few decades, she would have quite shamelessly seduced him and he would have been powerless to resist. Alexandra rarely failed to snare her prey, although she conceded that it was a bit beyond her now. What a pity. He looked so innocent and she thought that he was ripe for her attention.

She wondered how this young Adonis faired in the gentle skill of lovemaking, but cynically concluded that the art of seduction was lost on the young today, for whom the whole process appeared to have had been stripped of its allure and mystery. The enticement and theatre of wooing and winning the opposite sex had been replaced by almost contractual and instant gratification. No preparation - no patience. That irritated her. Boys worshipped magazine and internet images and girls might as well go about with signs on their backs, 'ready for rutting'. Subtlety seemed to be the victim of the new age.

Her thoughts were interrupted by an attractive olive skinned girl with beautiful almond eyes who smiled at her and held out a cup of tea. Returning her smile Alexandra thanked her, thinking of all those lovely people she had known in Surinam, formerly Dutch Guyana. She didn't know the girl's name, but she reminded her of the servants from those halcyon days in the Americas where she had lived with her parents who owned a plantation. It was a pleasant recollection and she closed her eyes for a moment recalling the beauty of the tropical forest that covered almost all of the country, with its humid hinterland and cool regions by lakes. It was a far cry from the orderliness of the Surrey Hills.

The tea was thin and almost tasteless, but her palate had not quite been up to the job recently so it didn't really matter. At least it quenched her thirst. The attention of the young lady in question had was far more satisfying, evoking as it did memories of days gone by. She had known such beautiful girls as servants, and once, as a lover. Not something everyone knew, but it was a secret that she guarded and brought out of its box to ponder over when times were hard. Being outrageous had always been her antidote to boredom or depression.

The noise around her was irritating. So many people, all bustling on their way to this and that. No one had time to say hello, or engage in meaningful and intelligent, or even amusing conversation. The thought struck her that she could be stark naked, because no one would damn well notice.

That triggered a pleasant memory and made her smile again. She closed her eyes quickly to capture the images before they melted away.

"Ah yes," she thought and breathed deeply.

Her first experience of the exhilaration of being without clothes had been when she was tempted to swim naked in a large lake near her home in Surinam. She had just reached seventeen years old and was experiencing the thrill of throwing off inhibitions and challenging the world about her.

As she stepped out of the water, she heard a dreadful racket from the rear of the house some two hundred metres from the lake. Used by now to her nakedness in the warm climate, she tiptoed unselfconsciously to the edge of the shrub that bordered the edge of the manicured lawn and looked across to the veranda to find out what was going on.

Her father had come back surprisingly early and was haranguing the local gardener. He was amusing when he was angry and it always made her laugh. His ruddy complexion would boil even more when he got upset and he sometimes repeated sentences, and that made even the most serious situation comic. She put it down to his grave Dutch character, although in truth there was nothing really continental about it, no more so than her mother's gaiety could be put down to her being an English rose. Then her father did something very strange. Quite out of character, he shouted and chased the man down the path waving his hands furiously. She watched as he ranted at the hapless gardener who was by now running in fear of his life. It later transpired that he had accidentally killed several of her father's prized roses, difficult to grow in the South American climate, by putting a strong dose of weed-killer on them.

The young Alexandra laughed at the scene in front of her, before languidly stretching her arms high above her head, feeling the cool air caress her body. As she turned to make her way back to her clothes by the lakeside, she saw a handsome young man walk onto the patio. She was transfixed. He was fair-haired and tall, dressed in a beige linen suit, over a white shirt and wore brown calf-length boots. It seemed that he was looking directly at her.

She recalled the strange feeling of excitement as she watched this handsome man from the private cover of the forest, move around the veranda; that recollection would stay with her for the rest of her life. Her throat tightened and she put her arms across the top of her body. All of a sudden, her heart jumped when she realised that they may all be tempted to search for the gardener in her part of the forest and she quickly scampered back to where her clothes lay at the lake-side.

She never got to meet the guest. Her father took him out to dinner and he left early the next day for a flight back to Germany. All she had left was the remnant of that sight of him, from the forest, before she dressed.

Alexandra moved awkwardly against the cushions behind her back, keeping her eyes tight shut, as she recalled how, for a long time after the incident, she relived this image over and over.

"Oh, to be young again," she thought.

The family home on the plantation estate in Surinam, named Randwyjk, after a small town near Maastricht in the South Limburg area of the Netherlands, held many memories for her. Alexandra was a privileged child and knew such innocent happiness. As she grew up, inevitably she was courted by a number of young men. Although many of them were considered to be quite a catch, none seemed to sustain her attention beyond a mild flirtation or game of tennis. None of them were ever able to compete with the vision of the house guest on the day of her swim.

Alexandra's innocence soon ended as her curiosity naturally led her to gain more experience. She learned to take the lead in any situation and that included the subtle art of controlling men. When the social atmosphere dimmed, Alexandra was always on hand to stoke the fire. As her parents aged, she held parties and was soon getting a reputation for outrageous behaviour. Several times, Alicia, one of the older Surinam servants who had known her since she was a very young child, would take her to one side and remind her of her responsibilities, but she didn't listen. Without the stimulation of day-to-day activity beyond boring schoolwork, it was difficult to pin down a girl like her. As far as she was concerned, life was for living and she would live it to the full. In a last hopeful gasp, her parents encouraged her to go to university in the UK. Alexandra jumped at the chance with alacrity, anything to get away from the humidity, the forests and the boredom of colonial life. Despite her anxiety to leave, the servants noticed a tear in her eye when she left the estate, looking back over her shoulder, through the tall gates towards the shuttered windows of the Randwyjk house, around which well trimmed wild creepers and vines held it in a tight embrace.

Alexandra remembered the excitement and expectation of life in the UK juxtaposed with the tug of emotion at leaving the family home.

The flight to London was a long one, transiting via North America in a BOAC Constellation, which at the time was the state of the art in aviation, with its four powerful propeller engines, long fuselage and curious large triple tail-fin. During the journey Alexandra had no trouble making friends, especially those of the opposite sex. By the time she reached her destination and had hauled her suitcases into her rooms at Bath University, she was an accomplished seductress with a collection of business cards. Released into a larger world she was determined to make the very most of it.

Her university years provided her with a literary degree and a talent for writing, which gave her entry into the world of novelists, poets and artists, gaining friendships with such notorious characters as Philip Larkin, Daphne du Maurier and Graham Green. They encouraged her writing, but above all, the need to question everything – it was, they said, a writer's profound duty. Unsurprisingly perhaps, they also sowed the seed that literary people

108

should lead the way on the subject of hedonism. She needed no encouragement and duly obliged.

Wherever she went, she challenged authority, particularly the assumptions made by men in what was a post-war male society. Sometimes she was outrageous and at other times eloquent and patient. In her approach to women's issues she was relentless. On other occasions, she went over the top and this sometimes led to short prison sentences. But her self-assurance always remained steady and unwavering, and in particular she became a champion for women who suffered from abuse by their partners. Most famously, she beat up a drunk who came looking for his battered and bruised wife, knocking several of his teeth out with a tennis racket. That earned her notoriety and a police caution.

The noise around her continued unabated. Despite a deep discomfort that was beginning to fill her body and the bustle of people around her, Alexandra continued to call up memories. It was a good antidote to pain as well as to boredom and besides, she suddenly felt she had to use this time to reminisce. She was filled with a kind of urgency.

Not all memories are pleasant. Her life in literary circles was selfish and in the haste to gain attention and have fun, she often forgot to write or call her long-suffering parents. It was easy to blame pressure of work, publishing deadlines, new book deals and all manner of things. London was far too exciting to leave, even for a week or so. Her parents missed her dreadfully. She failed to acknowledge it – pushing it to the back of her mind – like many young people bursting on to a new and exciting world, she thought that her parents would go on forever, would always be there and nothing would change. Living in the twilight zone that successful and energetic younger people live in was exciting – it was timeless, frozen, focussed and hypnotic. Back in Surinam, her father and mother began to think that they would never see her again.

Then, quite suddenly, her mother died from a fever she caught working to help local people in a housing project. Full of remorse Alexandra called her father who, grief stricken and angry at her previous lack of contact, feigned sickness and was unable to talk to her. She knew he was angry. To further shatter her life, he died within the week, taking his own life with a single gunshot to the head, unable to live without the woman he loved. She realised, only then, that she had never really stopped for long enough to develop a relationship with them both. Her mother had always been so loving, nurturing and caring, without a single bad characteristic, but busy with motherly chores and good causes. Her father had appeared irascible and full of humour to everyone but her. It was only when she took time to trawl through memories that she recalled the sounds of laughter from dinner parties and the way other men used to defer to him or laugh at his jokes, that she realised how little she really knew him. He must have truly loved her mother to end his life so suddenly and in such a way.

Alexandra felt a sharp stab of pain to her heart as she thought about this. How easy it had been to be taken on the conveyor belt of life that led from one success to another, one party to another, one man to another. Forgetting all too easily that there were others who had always been there for her. Now it was too late. She rubbed her chest to try and suppress the piercing pains and returned to her thoughts to take her mind off them.

The year after their death, during which time she suffered a nervous breakdown, had been the worst of her life. Introspection caused her to create such enormous guilt that she was unable to work or behave rationally. After losing most of her friends, she descended into self-pity and depression and, predictably, drifted into alcoholism; thankfully she avoided drugs.

It was fellow novelist, Charles Danberry, who picked her up and put her together again. As she recalled his face Alexandra smiled. They had two children and divorced after fifteen years. Although it was too short a span of time, this part of her life had then been the most settled, during which she wrote several best selling novels. One was entitled, "Lost Hearts", a fictional story, full of references, about a girl who grows up to be a successful businesswoman in New York and forgets her family who disown her and the effect of guilt on her life thereafter. She also wrote a non-fiction novel on Surinam's history under Dutch rule and the country's rise to independence. Her work-rate increased to fever pitch which was what caused the split from her husband Charles.

In the years that followed she began to take on her old persona and headed for the party scenes. This threw the children, Lilly and Jason, towards their father. Funnily enough, no one seemed to mind. She had produced offspring with a little of her own DNA and they resolutely got on with their lives and let her get on with hers. It is perhaps true that family characteristics and mistakes are simply socialised in one generation after another. Even after the divorce, everything was quite amicable and contact between them all was more ad hoc, than planned.

In her fifties, she, like many other men and women, felt that time was sliding by quicker than ever and that there was more to be done and to be experienced. This spurred her on to reach out for any passing flotsam and jetsam of an idea or project. She set up trust funds for the advancement of women's studies, became one of the first female independent Member of Parliament. After that failed to satisfy her, she resigned in a flurry of media hype and went to Africa to harangue both white South African and black states alike for their stupidity and selfishness. Her efforts to change that continent had little impact and it was rumoured that friends drugged her and had her flown to safety in the UK before she was to be imprisoned. It was perhaps in the depths of her second round of depression that she met a younger man, Raymond Purcell, in whom she confided and sought comfort in a moment of rare weakness.

He was a charlatan and the only man to ever take advantage of her financially or in any other way, and by the time she realised it, he had emptied her accounts and she was penniless. But it brought her back to life. Alexandra was not a woman to be reckoned with. It was never proved, but one night, mysteriously and without motive, two men kidnapped and beat Purcell senseless and broke his legs. He would never walk or feed himself again.

Alexandra kept his photograph in the downstairs toilet, in a cheap frame, upside down, for the rest of her life as an indictment to her stupidity. She settled in a small flat in Redhill, Surrey and although poorer, continued to write novels and short stories. Her cats provided her with all the companionship she needed. They were undemanding and quite unlikely to rob her or let her down. Only her memories played havoc with her mind, but she could usually sort these out.

The commotion around her was again beginning to make her angry and she knew that she had to keep herself calm. As she became more agitated, her heart beat faster and her temperature rose, flashbacks occurred, coming from left and right, in different forms, presenting sometimes awful pictures, the kind that make one want to shout out with fear or anger for a loved one's safety or other terrible event. The pace of the flashbacks increased like a cinema newsreel playing at four times the speed. Almost every painful event from her past seemed to be raining down on her, there were hardly any nice thoughts now. Reliving the fact that that she knew as little about her husband and children, as she did about her parents, made her chest tighten and a deep sadness descend on her. The vision of her mother came to mind from the left then it peeled away and was replaced by her father's face, ruddy, but frowning. Her eyes moistened and she became determined not to let people around her see her crying - she had never ever allowed anyone to see her weak and vulnerable and was not going to do so now. She clenched her eyes shut and her knuckles went white as she tightened her hands together.

"Drown it out – drown out the bloody noise and commotion", she thought. She would have to concentrate hard and it would all go away, and so would the pain she felt in her chest as the memories chipped away at her soul.

"Oh God, for a gin or two, right now," she thought.

Alexandra ached for the numbness that comes with alcoholic oblivion, anything would be welcome to remove the unwanted visions of the past, the necessity to be judged and feel guilt, and the commotion of the present – and this damned pain in her chest.

Then her head began to swirl. A familiar and hurtful dream began to form in front of her. It was impossible to stop it and this time it was all the more vivid and bright. In it she was walking up a jungle pathway to the house, Randwyjk, but it was terribly overgrown with weeds and sometimes the path itself was lost in the mess of greenery. The path meandered and she walked on slowly through scenery that she thought she had forgotten since her childhood. She knew in her heart that she wanted to be a little girl again and see Alicia, the Surinam servant who guided her through childhood, but failed with her adolescence. Even after her parents died Alexandra had not returned to Randwyjk and it left a big guilty hole in her heart. People who knew her at the plantation never forgave her - at least she thought that they didn't.

The gates came into view and although she had never ever seen them closed during her childhood, they were now. A giant shiny brass padlock clenched itself around the wrought iron gate-latch. Through the gate she could see Randwyjk, dilapidated, overgrown with creepers and vines, the paintwork shabby and peeling, windows and plantation shutters dirty, some of them broken and the roof in disorder.

She caught her breath as she stared at the shimmering vision in front of her. Her mother, father and Alicia came into view, standing to the left of the house. But as she desperately tried to talk to them no words came. It was always the same. No words came and her throat hurt with nervous strain. Worse still, they looked at her as though she didn't exist; only Alicia seemed to see her, but she just turned away. The hurt was almost unbearable. She wanted to explain, to say sorry, and tell them all about her life and the fact that she had always been driven to succeed and sometimes to be outrageous. To tell them what she had achieved, as well admitting to her made mistakes. How she wanted to talk to them all and seek their forgiveness.

In the background, she could see all her old friends were walking around seemingly looking for something, searching everywhere. Then as if from nowhere, the shouts of young children could be heard and she saw Lilly and Jason, young and fresh faced children, dressed in summer clothes, not the independent and indifferent adults that they had grown into. They stopped and looked at her and after a few moments they too turned away shouting for their father. This scene always upset her.

The vision was always the same. Why? It wasn't fair. She had put more into her life than any other lacklustre soul she knew. Why couldn't the world keep up with her? Everyone has to forge out a life for themselves – everyone. So why did it always come to this? In the vision, her tears fell from her cheeks, but no one seemed to notice and, distressingly, no one appeared to care. But this time, it was different and it hurt her even more than it had ever done before, her body ached with emotion.

113

Gradually, a quiet ringing sounded in her ears, slowly increasing in volume and all of a sudden the dull hurt in her chest receded and all physical discomfort and pain vanished. The noises and clamour around her faded and a bright light enveloped her forming a kind of swirling tunnel. Along the tunnel she could see the path to Randwyjk again, this time clear of debris and lined with wild yellow irises that grew in the cool reed-lands to the left of the plantation and she willingly propelled herself along it. To her delight and joy the gates to the house were now wide open and as she looked at her old family home she saw that it was brightly painted. There were green leaves and well trimmed vines around the windows.

Her feet carried her smoothly, floating, through the gates and towards the house and she saw, left and right, her mother and father, Alicia the servant, her husband Charles and the children, and all her friends and acquaintances. But now, they were all smiling and waving. They beckoned her towards them. She felt enormous overwhelming happiness and reached out to touch them, tears streaming down her face – it was all over. She could talk to them and explain her life and everything was going to be all right at last. They could share and talk at last and everything would all be all right. She felt overwhelming joy.

Then the light shone, gradually getting even brighter, eventually obscuring everything.

Doctor Jonathon Roberts, stood behind senior consultant, Mister Julian Harris, as he felt for Alexandra Van Der Klerk's pulse. He was in a hurry and it showed.

"Okay. That's it I'm afraid. She's dead. Time of death, let's say, eleven thirty three A.M. Put it down please as a 'death in bed'," he swivelled at looked at Doctor Roberts adding, "not a 'trolley death,' Jonathon. Look see, no wheels, gotta keep the stats straight, eh?"

Jonathon Roberts looked at all the trolleys lined up in the corridor waiting to be allocated bed spaces, they were all minus wheels so that the low statistic signifying 'trolleys waiting to be allocated a bed space,' could be ticked without reservation. They weren't trolleys, they were beds. Two hospital janitors fitted the wheels back on the trolley and Alexandra's body was covered with a sheet and taken directly to a mortuary. He stared at the bed, now a trolley, as it was quickly wheeled away, shortening the queue of people awaiting allocation of bed spaces on wards. He was grateful that those remaining in the queue were asleep or sedated.

Jonathon was sad she had died. He knew she was over eighty and a famous novelist. Only the twinkle in her eyes had betrayed her as someone with a little more about her than some of the other elderly people he looked after. As he was about to leave, he looked down and noticed a book lying on the floor. He picked it up and read the title, "Lost Hearts." As he flipped through the pages, a photograph almost fell to the floor. He caught it and looked at the sepia image. It was of a large house, the type often found on colonial plantations, with large shuttered windows and verandas. In front of it was a pair of large white stone gateposts holding half-open black wrought iron gates.

On one of the gateposts was a sign saying, Randwyjk.

# AU BOIS (To the Woods)

The sun was rising over the Devon town of Ivybridge, dispersing the light mists that slid down from the moorland, giving the countryside a bright yellow glow. It had been glorious weather the day before and promised more of the same for the coming day. The police station was situated behind the new shopping precinct and was modern and not at all like its old-fashioned red brick predecessor that had now long since been demolished. Inside, there was a small, modern waiting room with bright blue plastic chairs, light blue floor tiles and two notice boards festooned with advice of all sorts, the most prominent advising householders about burglaries in the local area, and to motorists, exhorting them not to drink and drive. A main reception desk was on the right hand side of the entrance. There were no metal bars or shatterproof screens; none were needed in small-town Ivybridge.

It was quiet and the station police officer, Sergeant Graham Swanley, had just arrived and was looking at some papers on his desk. A young constable was standing with his hands behind his back and a smirk on his face. He had that, 'aiming to impress' look, which the sergeant was trying to ignore. Swanley had seen probationers like this come and go and Constable Jenkins tried his patience more than most.

In the interview room sat an attractive auburn haired woman in her mid forties, calmly reading a book, with her feet up on the bench seat. Her male companion paced the room and was very agitated, walking up and down muttering to himself. The woman carried on reading, unperturbed, smiling quietly to herself.

At the reception desk, Sergeant Swanley looked over his spectacles, regarding the young constable as one would a school prefect reporting a classmate for some minor misdemeanour.

"Well let's see then. The offence, if that's what it is, took place in an area adjacent to the Golf Club, is that right?

The constable straightened up. "Yes, sarge, that's right, the Ugbury Golf Club to be precise."

Sniffing loudly, the sergeant continued. "Tell me, just why were you in the woods at that time of the night, Jenkins?"

Oblivious to the sergeant's curiosity, he replied, nonchalantly, "Patrolin' sarge. That's my job. I drive around looking for suspicious goin's on."

Staring at him, the sergeant waited a few seconds before asking, "Yes, but why Jenkins, why? It's well off your normal route. Can I remind you, that you are not 'looking for trade' so to speak, but merely there to reassure the public, warn off criminals and react when called upon?"

"Well, er, I just do what my instincts tell me sarge. I drive around and if I see anything suspicious then, I follow it up."

The sergeant harrumphed at the feigned modesty and turned to sarcasm.

"Regular little Poirot aren't we?"

The constable looked hurt and the sergeant continued, "and talking of 'instincts', isn't that what *they* were doin'," he nodded towards the interview room, "what comes naturally that is?"

"Yes, sarge. But it is against the law. The Home Secretary is very strict on that. It's the law, well the government's. Banning such lewd action in a public place and ..." the sergeant cut him off.

"Jenkins, this was hardly the edge of a school playground, café or bus stop. Now, pray tell me, as if we don't have enough jobs to do around the community, just for the report, where were they precisely and at what time did this incident occur?"

Unruffled by the sergeant's apparent lack of interest, the constable referred to his notebook, flicking through the pages like a busy bank clerk facing the task of counting a million pounds in five-pound notes. Then he found the page he wanted and, demonstrably stabbing his finger at it, he thought for a moment and said, "At precisely, er, two minutes past midnight. As I said in the report it was by the Ugbury Golf Course, to the left, there is a small car park and a path into the woods. That's where I saw the shoes – red sling backs I think they are called – by the car. A Jaguar car. Very posh, erm, well, that's what caught my eye."

"Go on."

"Well, a short way in to the wood there's a large holly tree – and there they were, sarge. I shone my torch on them and said loudly, 'What's goin' on 'ere?' "

The sergeant looked at the ceiling as if in a daze.

"Yes, well, hardly a fair question really. So then, was it a case of coitus interruptus?"

"Coytus-inter-what-tus sarge?

"Interruptus, Jenkins, interruptus. For goodness sake, had they 'finished' what they were doing constable, had they finished?"

"Oh, er, I don't rightly know sarge."

"No, silly question I suppose, I doubt if you would."

The constable missed the barb and the sergeant tapped his teeth with his pencil.

"Let's put it another way, let me think, ah yes. Were they movin' Jenkins, movin'?"

"Oh, er, no sarge, come to think of it they were completely still. That's right, still, not movin' at all."

"Then, please explain why you found it necessary to arrest them and save the nation's blushes?"

"Ah! Well it was clear to me sarge that they had been at it, so to speak. Yes, for certain. His trousers were down below his knees and her clothes were sort of, dishevelled."

The constable's voice tailed off as though he didn't want to go into any more detail.

"Dishevelled, well that's a good word. Let's move on then, painfully I admit, but onwards and upwards as they say. Jenkins, was there evidence of complicity on both sides in the act?"

"Sorry, sarge?"

The sergeant snapped, "Were they bloody smiling' Jenkins?"

"Oh! I see what you mean sarge. Yes, they were both complicit. But they weren't both smiling'. She was but he wasn't."

"I can't wait, go on."

"Well, she smiled and sort of, fluffed his hair and called him a name?"

"A name, Jenkins?"

"Yes, sarge."

"Please, Jenkins, I want to finish this report before I get my pension!"

"Tiger. That's it – she said, well, er," he referred to his notebook again. "That was lovely my darling, Tiger! That was it, Tiger. I remember now."

"Strewth! We really are plumbing the depths of public morality here aren't we? Okay, what then?"

"Well sarge, as I was shining my torch at them, the man jumps up and immediately falls over, his trousers you see_" the sergeant interrupted.

"So he did a Norman Wisdom did he," obviously pleased with his interjection.

"_yes, sarge, anyway, the lady just laughed. She laughed a lot while she was adjusting her clothes. In fact she laughed all the way to the cars and seemed not to care that I was cautioning them. He, the man that is, wanted her to take it all very seriously and was very distressed. The man, Mr Alerdyce, remonstrated with her to stop and to grow up."

"Mr Alerdyce, eh? The new manager at Marchant's Bank and esteemed captain of the Ugbury Golf Club. Well, well," he chuckled and gazed ahead, thinking of his overdraft and the way the bank had recently written reminding him of it.

"I suppose you could say that he made a small deposit and withdrew having lost significant interest," he continued to chuckle, "and having tarried with the 'footsie', he has to tidy up his assets."

He laughed some more and it became obvious to Constable Jenkins that his boss was momentarily oblivious to anything more than enjoying his own crude humour and the embarrassment of the local bank manager.

Sergeant Swanley reached for a mug of tea and sipped it loudly, gathered his wits and said, "Ahem, right then, Jenkins, do you still want to proceed with a charge against these two people?"

"Of course sarge. It's the law sarge and our duty to uphold it – to the letter."

Exasperated, the sergeant flapped the papers on his desk.

"Okay then, that will be all for now. Take this report form and fill it in. Let me have it back in an hour."

In the interview room, Lawrence Alerdyce had finally stopped pacing. They had opted to stay the night in the police station because of his anger at being arrested. He was damned if he was going home with a caution against his name for something so embarrassing and unnecessary. It was all a storm in a teacup and his lawyer would sort it out. This would be sorted out or he would camp out in the station until it was. He talked to himself out loud.

"Why? What in hell's name came over me? This is so acutely embarrassing. I can see our friends, our neighbours – oh yes, they will have a laugh at my, no, *our* expense. Oh God! And Fothergill the district manager, he'll have a field day, he has always been a bit iffy about me."

Lawrence raised his balled hands in front of him as if in defence, then, exasperated, he dropped them by his side and harrumphed loudly. "Well, now he has his chance. Damnation!"

There was a knock at the door, which he found profoundly stupid since this was supposed to be the modern equivalent of a medieval gaol and not a hotel room. It was Sergeant Swanley.

"Mr Alerdyce, sorry to disturb you sir, but I just wanted to check that you were all right. You weren't arrested last night sir, but if you recall you were, well, too distraught to continue your journey home. We do however need to clarify the situation before, er, well thinking about, well, charges sir. But let's fix you up with some tea and breakfast and can I advise you to call a friend or solicitor. You can use the phone at the desk, dial nine for an outside line."

"Sergeant, thank you but for the record I opted to stay because this has been a travesty of justice. As for a lawyer, mobile telephones enable the more quick-witted to call their lawyers and I have already done just that." Exhausted and tired, he softened. "Actually, a cup of tea and some toast would go down a treat. Thank you. And I guess I had better follow up my earlier call. So I will take you up on your offer to use your telephone."

Lawrence left the room, not knowing whether to be angry with the well-meaning sergeant or grateful for his concern. As he left the room he said, "Oh, woe is me. Thank you for your consideration, it's not your fault, I know. See you in a minute Jane."

He left his wife Jane and the sergeant together and went out into the waiting area, ignoring Constable Jenkins who was diligently filling in a number of forms and didn't look up.

Sergeant Swanley couldn't help being a little in awe of Jane Alerdyce, imagining what it must have been like lying with this lovely attractive lady under a holly tree on a starry night. He thought her quite beautiful and his eyes strayed. Feeling his gaze Jane looked up, lazily straightening her legs and clothing. He coughed and looked embarrassed.

"Is there anything you'd like, Mrs Alerdyce?" he said, with a half-sloppy smile that might grace the face of a schoolboy with a crush on a teacher.

She stretched and yawned, then smiled at him and he actually felt his heart beat faster, "No. No thank you sergeant. I think I am really just fine."

Sergeant Swanley clasped his hands together, fingers entwined and Jane thought how he looked a little like Dickens' character, Uriah Heep.

"Look, I am not really supposed to say this," he said, and he half sat on the bench, which she found a tad familiar. "I am truly sorry that we have to pursue this matter. I mean, a nice lady like you shouldn't have to answer silly questions. You know about, well, this and that."

He put his hands on his knees and looked distinctly uncertain about what he was about to say, like a little boy getting ready to tell his teacher that he had piddled himself. He squinted and put on a supercilious expression.

"I mean, it is a bit embarrassing, isn't it?"

Jane looked straight at him and shifted her position so that both her feet were together on the bench, with her arms around her knees.

"The process won't take long mind you, but, well we will have to corroborate certain, er, things, in the report if you know what I mean. I hope you don't mind me saying, we are about the same age I would guess, it was a bit of an odd place to er, well..." and his voice trailed off leaving the rest of his sentence unsaid.

Jane continued to smile at him and slowly put the book down on the bench.

"Tell me, Sergeant, when and where did you last pleasure Mrs Plod?"

Sergeant Swanley stood up quickly.

"Mrs Alerdyce, that's quite and improper question!"

"Maybe, sergeant, but if you don't ask me about my sex life, I won't ask you about yours, is that a deal?"

Sergeant Swanley was at a loss for words and indignantly turned and walked out of the room. Jane grinned broadly. This was getting to be so much fun.

Lawrence came back into the interview room, almost bumping past the sergeant as he did so.

He smiled at her. "That's it, all done. James got my mobile message and is on his way. He's a good lawyer and if anyone can sort this out he can, you'll see. Everything will be okay." He rubbed his hands nervously.

Jane stared at him enigmatically and a dozen questions formed on her lips – but she decided to let matters take their course. It would be time to talk very soon. She picked up her book absentmindedly and began to read again.

Lawrence spoke restlessly. "I still don't understand what came over me. One minute I'm having a quiet coffee and saying goodbye to the Golf Club guests and the next I feel, well, erm, aroused and then we are in the bloody woods, doing it. Crikey. I'm a sex maniac. God, me, of all people. I mean, I didn't know what a 'johnny' was until I was nineteen and I never bought dirty magazines, in fact I was pretty sexually blameless as an adolescent. And now? I'll be shunned by society, people will lock up their daughters."

Jane stifled her laughter; this was just too funny – embarrassing yes, but also so very funny. A mobile phone rang and she reached into her handbag and, without looking up from her book, handed it to a surprised Lawrence.

"It's probably the News of the World," she said with a grin.

Lawrence blanched. "Oh heck, don't say that," he put the mobile to his ear,

"Hello, yes? Oh, Gill, darling. No everything is okay. Just a spot of bother. Ah, right, so you know? How did you bloody well know? Oh, James! I'll kill him, he's my lawyer not my brother, who else knows? Crikey, the kids – well, so they were worried, so what? I've spent the last decade worrying about them staying out all night – let me tell you, it's no big deal!"

After a few minutes he grew agitated. "Okay, okay, that's enough of that, it's not funny, Gill. No, Gill, it wasn't like that."

As he wrestled for words Jane giggled to herself behind her book.

"Look, I've had enough of this," he continued, "I'll pass your kind wishes to Jane and she'll call you. No I am not being sensitive, thank you, Gill, and no I will not give Charles any tips, goodbye!"

He pressed the red button on the mobile and looked at Jane.

"That was your sister. So the ridicule begins. She thought the family might be worried, how disingenuous is that? You know, of course, what will happen? Within the next fifteen minutes she will have told your mother," he groaned, "the chemist, the ladies in the supermarket and anyone else who will listen. She is of course delighted at our situation. But why not? She never quite forgave me for catching her out, snogging her son's math's teacher at a sports day some years back, you remember? We had to keep that secret from Charles. Oh yes, she'll love this! What's more, I can do without her saying that she didn't think I had it in me – she made a lewd comment - about lead and pencils!"

Lawrence stared at the ceiling and moments later the mobile phone rang again. He looked at it, considered not answering, but changed his mind, and reached for it sulkily.

"Yes. Hello, darling. Look, don't worry about a thing…what…? Of course not, your mum and I do not make a habit of getting into trouble with the law…don't be rude Gabrielle…that either! It's not what you think. No. No…please, do not tell your friends. Okay, okay, I know where you are coming from Gabrielle. The new wind-surfing sail you want – it's yours if you don't…hello, hello…Gabrielle?"

Jane put her fingers to her mouth stifling yet another laugh. Gabrielle played her father like a violin and was adept at spotting a business opportunity.

"What did she have to say darling?"

"She rang off. Apparently, she is as happy as a sparrow. She thinks we are so cool." Lawrence turned and looked at Jane. "So, that's it then, forget that you are chair of the local Women's Institute and I am a successful bank manager, school governor and chairman of this and that. No, that is plain boring stuff. Now, this is the coolest thing we have ever done. Crikey, if only I had known how easy it would be to get myself admired by my kids I would have behaved so much more irresponsibly throughout my life."

He sat down heavily on the bench and Jane reached out and touched his hand lightly. The mobile rang again. Lawrence was by now past caring

"Hello, Ugbury resident sex maniac speaking." He paused and added quickly, "Oh God, Fothergill, sorry my dear chap, just, er, joking. What can I do for you?"

He listened for a few seconds and Jane was intrigued.

"Well thank you, it was a fine dinner and a good fundraising event too, the Golf Club certainly did do us proud. I trust you were happy with the choice of pro-golfer for tomorrow, sorry, today's match? I am not sure that I will make the T-off time. No we can't meet this morning I am a bit tied up. Jane? Oh she's fine and how is your good lady?"

Lawrence began to look a little worried and drew his cheeks back, screwing his face up. "Oh crikey, did I? Please do tell her that I was feeling, well, very happy, and frankly it was the excitement of a successful evening and…"

His voice trailed off as he listened intently, then said, "Oh really? Well, that is very, er, sporting of her. I hope she wasn't offended? Oh, far from it. Yes, right, thank you for saying so. See you later perhaps. Bye for now."

Lawrence turned the mobile off and threw it on to the bench.

"I'm in a mad dream! He was amused! She was amused! I am becoming a new person." He looked at Jane forlornly as if helpless to the situation unfolding around him. "Apparently I cuddled his wife Suzie and playfully twanged her bra strap. Far from being upset they thought me a real 'player' and Suzie in particular was amused. He had a good laugh and you know what? They didn't want 'me' to feel awkward 'the morning after'. He sees me in a new light – crikey, double-crikey, the world's going mad!"

124

Jane was by now rubbing his arm. The situation had turned out better than she thought. Should she tell him now, or what?

"Jane, I am so sorry, I..."

Jane reached out and touched his lips and stopped him speaking any more.

"Why? What for? It was simply glorious, you were glorious! You...we...were great. We were twenty-something all over again. And you're sorry?"

Lawrence was a little taken aback.

"Put like that, I suppose...but...well, it's the entire furore..."

"There we have it. The furore eh? What is it that worries you more, a dent in your pride or the way you let yourself go? You know, you've done so well in your life Lawrence, but I want to tell you something without hurting you: in some aspects of life you have become a bit of a bore."

"A bore!" he spluttered.

"Yes, do you want me to explain?"

"Please do, things can't get any worse!"

"You're one of the best, Lawrence, we have virtually grown up together and enjoyed many things in life. Do you remember when you played Santa Claus one Christmas when we lived in Camberley? You finished your evening rounds and thought it a hoot to strip off, then put the suit back on before coming in to the living room – you wanted to give me a 'Christmas surprise' under the tree? The only problem was that I had asked the neighbours in for a seasonal drink."

Lawrence fought back laughter, but didn't succeed very well and they both dissolved.

"Yes, yes, I do indeed. Oh, how close it was to me making a grand entrance," then they laughed some more. "Oh yes. I do remember. The poor Spencers didn't know why I wouldn't sit down – the middle button on the robe was a bit unreliable if you recall? And you, you little minx, when you realised you kept giving me the come on. There could've been quite a nasty accident mid-sherry."

"Precisely," she said and touched his hair, brushing his quiff off his forehead. "That's just it. I truly love you darling, but we seem to have lost that fun in our lives. I am not suggesting that we bonk on the village square, but we could try and reclaim some of our passion

– make much more time for ourselves. Whatever happened to fish and chips, and Champagne in the bath?"

"Ah! Now I do feel rotten. I know that I've not been, well, er...."

Jane reached out and touched his lips again, just as tenderly.

"Don't think I don't understand. Success brings with it stress and all that jazz. I know. How can you turn on passion and be the 'Don Juan' when you are under pressure at work. For eight to ten hours a day you sit on your best parts, no wonder they've been squashed into complete submission. But, I am being selfish for the first time in my life. I need to confess that I took the opportunity to encourage and guide you last night and it worked.

"You're so lovely, but I am beginning to feel a little less manly as this conversation goes on."

"Then you're not listening. Get rid of the testosterone gremlin that sits on most men's shoulders. If I challenged you and said to you that I wanted you to bed me more often you would have run a mile. Women have to suffer the music hall jokes and the slings and arrows of chemical changes to their bodies – but when the going gets tough on the romance front for you chaps, you get moody and sulk. It's life, Lawrence, and I just want us both to get the most out of it, that's reasonable isn't it?"

He smiled at her, noticing her eyes were still as brown and warm as when he first met her.

"I guess I see what you are saying. I never had you down for pushy broad. But where is this going Jane, how did I do what I did. I was pretty high on gin, but not that bad? One minute I am saying goodbye to guests and the next moment I twang bra straps and you're kissing me, wow! My God it was a close shave. I mean snogging in the car right outside the Golf Club, I hope no one saw us, I just had to drive away, and, yes, I remember now. You threw your bloody underwear at me!"

Jane laughed out loud.

"Then I take fright and drive to the car park next door to the Club and we end up, well, in the woods. In fact you pulled me there! The rest is history."

Lawrence looked exasperated, then took Jane by the shoulders and looked straight into her eyes.

"Beautiful history as I recall, it was rather good wasn't it?"

They sat for a while smiling at each other.

"But how...I just don't understand...?"

Jane smiled, reached into her handbag and pulled out a box, which rattled as she did so. She opened it and took out a blue triangular tablet and held it between her finger and thumb. Lawrence stared in disbelief.

"Close your mouth, Lawrence, you look like a sloppy Labrador. Well, go on have a look at it, it's not a blue asprin you dope!"

"My God, it's Viag...."

Jane raised her hand. "Yes. So what?"

"But that's for men who..."

Jane interrupted. "Oh for goodness sake, dispense with the gremlin. That's not the case. It's just another item for the bedroom tool-kit."

She let out a peel of laughter. "If you'll forgive the unintended pun! It's not a 'failure' pill, merely an enhancer, an encourager, an aid, that's all."

Lawrence held the pill up to the light as if he were trying to work out its magical properties, and then tossed it back to Jan.

"Okay," he sat down heavily on the bench and looked sheepishly at her, "there really is no disputing the effect. I did feel, well, rather excitable. I don't suppose you noticed that towards the end of the evening I had my Jacket done up quite a lot and didn't stand up much?"

"I did!" she said.

"Oh crikey. But how did I take one of those, er, thingys?"

"Easy peasy, you always take a glass of sparkling water with your coffee. I popped it in when you weren't looking and halved the amount of water so that you would drink it all. Simple really."

Lawrence smiled, "And...?"

Jane gazed at him, smiling.

"It has to be said, Tiger, my Tiger. You started to look extremely uneasy after about seventeen minutes." She held up the box and looked at the label. Frankly, it should say that in the directions for use. Fothergill was right, you did get pretty saucy. I must say though, this furore wasn't planned and I'm really sorry for that, darling."

Lawrence leaned back against the wall and thought for a few seconds. "I guess I have been a bit of a chump, a fool even."

Jane sprang up and knelt on the bench close to him.

"But not to me, not to me..." then she pounced on him and their lips met, tightly and passionately as they embraced.

A light knock on the door made them look up and Constable Jenkins entered. On seeing them firmly embraced, he tripped and dropped the tray with its tea and toast on the floor. Flummoxed, he left the room without bothering to clear up the mess, shouting, "Sarge, blimey sarge, they're at it again!"

Lawrence and Jane were startled at first, and then they burst into laughter.

At the reception desk the Sergeant Swanley was talking to a tall, distinguished looking man wearing a dark suit and a grey overcoat with a black felt collar, as Constable Jenkins hopped from foot to foot, unsure what to do with himself. Sergeant Swanley looked sideways with disdain as he said, "Sorry about that, sir. Constable Jenkins is apt to get a little excited. Do go in to the room, sir, I'll get someone to clear up the mess."

James Claybourn, Lawrence's solicitor smiled beguilingly, "Thank you so very much sergeant, most kind of you, I do appreciate it."

The sergeant straightened up, glad to be appreciated by someone of status in the legal profession.

James went into the interview room. As he put his head around the door he saw Lawrence and Jane still locked in an embrace, oblivious to the world around them.

"Ahem! I 'm not sure what you're smoking, Lawrence, but can I have some?"

Lawrence and Jane uncoupled and looked up at him in surprise.

"Ah, James, thanks for coming old chap. What a mess, this is all very embarrassing. The police have got it all wrong. I, we, are innocent. This is quite awful."

James looked at the ceiling in mock disgust.

"Don't be such a nerd, Lawrence. Most men I know would be jolly envious." He smiled at Jane who tried to look coy, but he wasn't fooled. "I've read Constable Jenkins' report and by Jove he does go into detail."

Jane got up and walked to the opposite wall.

James frowned playfully and said, "I thought boxer shorts were definitely a thing of the past?"

Jane raised her eyebrows. "And stockings and suspenders?"

He smiled at the way she was dealing with the situation and said laughingly, "Ho ho, m'lud, it's all here in black and white."

Lawrence returned to his indignant self. "Okay you two, let's please concentrate on what's to be done to get us out of this mess."

Noticing that they were both giggling like school children he said, "Oh, what the hell, I'm off for a pee."

When he had gone, James faced Jane.

"God...I wish I were Lawrence!

"Thank you. But you're not, and we dealt with that before I married him. You're still our best friend and always will be."

"Yes," he replied, resignedly looking towards the half open door, "and it has to be said, jealous but happy to be so. Let's get down to business. I don't want to know the 'whys' that's for you and your man to sort out. What's your story?"

"Simple. I playfully popped a little blue pill in to Lawrence sparkling water last night at the Golf Club Pro-Am dinner. I waited the requisite time then rigorously seduced him under a lovely holly tree in the woods by the club."

She raised two hands with imaginary pistols in each and pointed them at James' loins. " Pow! Without mercy!"

"I say, it's hard to argue with that. So what time did this all happen?"

"Well, not counting the foreplay?"

"Jane, you little devil be serious for just a minute will you?"

"Oh, if I must, James. Look, don't think badly of us, it was truly lovely and although amused, I am sorry that it all got out of hand, because we were spotted. Anyway, we embraced for some time and then it got a bit wild. I guess it was about, let's see, just after midnight and we settled under a large holly tree, to, er, be nice to each other. After about forty minutes or so, 'PC prurient' pounced. Yes that's it, I remember the time accurately, because I couldn't stop laughing, because as he shone his torch on us I looked at my watch. For some reason thought of him as some kind of comic ghost who sets out to punish evil fornicators."

James looked thoughtful. "Midnight plus forty minutes you say, are you perfectly sure?"

"Yes, absolutely and by the way, I would do it again you know James."

For a moment James was lost in his own thoughts as he fumbled through a handful of papers and he didn't answer straight away.

"Yes, Jane, I am sure you would – ever the free spirit. Jane will you excuse me for just a minute?"

Leaving his coat and briefcase on the bench he left the interview room with the police report in his hand.

After about five minutes Lawrence came back with his hands in his pockets.

"Okay then. Did you spill the beans? He's always fancied you, you know? Probably thinks that I'm useless and unworthy of you. Anyway, he's going hammer and tongs at the station sergeant and the constable looks a bit sheepish. I wonder what that's all about."

Jane walked towards Lawrence and took him by the hand. "I don't know. He rushed off with the report papers. Listen to me. I would never let you down Lawrence, so stop being sorry for yourself. He thinks it was a prank on my part. And whilst we are at it, I don't care if you are operated by clockwork, I just want you up close, loving and very personal. I love you and need you, and only you, very much indeed."

They embraced tenderly and were about to kiss when James came in.

"Goodness gracious me, my dear friends, do you never stop?"

Lawrence and Jane laughed sheepishly and separated.

"Well, dear hearts, the good news is that there are no charges whatsoever. So you can go home and have a cuppa, then get ready for a splendid Charity Golf Day, Lawrence. Enjoy it, you deserve it. That is of course if you two can stop coupling for just a while longer?" He winked theatrically and angled his head at the pair of them.

"This act of brilliance on my part does of course mean that at T-off today, I get to be paired with that lovely lady, you know the one, the UK Open Champion, Sylvia, 'what's her name?' Blonde and voluptuous, and a great swinger, I understand. I think that's the least you can do. In fact, do that and I will waive my fee – fair?"

Lawrence beamed. "Wow! Great stuff, what a relief. Yes, fair it is, James, buddy, I will certainly see what I can do. But how did you do it?"

James pushed his chest out. "Never you mind, too much detail, be off with you sir!"

"Righty ho, great, oh I feel so much better. I guess I must sign out or do something official at the desk, I'll do that now. Jane, you gather up our stuff and I will catch up at the entrance."

"Yes darling," she said, half turning to James, as Lawrence almost bounced out of the room.

"Okay, James, spill the beans."

"Ah. Well, I didn't want to embarrass poor Lawrence, he's the sensitive sort. It was something you said about being sprung upon at forty or so minutes past midnight. PC prurient had put in his report that he happened upon you both at about midnight, and that means he, well, how shall I put this politely. He hung around over that forty minute period. I told a fib and said that it would be easy to corroborate your statement with support from guests departing the club who told me that they saw the police car leaving the Golf Club car park at eleven fifty and proceeding to the wooded area moments after that."

He smiled and was obviously pleased with himself.

"The constable isn't that bright and he quickly admitted to spending quite some time 'observing' you both. I rather think that it is going to turn out that his nocturnal patrols were not all that he said they were. I think he will be leaving his patrol car soon for a desk job for a while. It seems his 'instincts' got the better of him as well!"

"Clever man, James. Thank you so much."

Jane pecked him on the cheek and after gathering up her and Lawrence's belongings they both left the interview room. The station sergeant and the constable pretended to busy themselves at the reception desk and barely looked up as they passed. Lawrence was just putting the top back on his pen having signed both him and Jane out of the station and looked very pleased with himself. He turned to her and smiled broadly.

"Okay, darling, let's go and celebrate with a late breakfast or brunch shall we?"

Jane looked at him, open-eyed and grinning, and raised her hand in which she held a small plastic box. She shook it vigorously and it rattled.

Lawrence's jaw dropped in surprise and his hands automatically covered his loins.

"Tick Tack mint, anyone?" she said smiling broadly.

They convulsed with laughter.

# Albert's Hands

Maisie sat by large French windows that were the centre-piece to her room and watched a small number of adults and children enjoying the sunshine on a large patch of grass in the garden outside. The early June sky was cloudless and warm. Although everyone enjoyed the warmth of summer some of the elderly and those with poor use of their arms, hated it. This was because plant spores matured then separated from the plant, floating skywards, filling the air like millions of small helium balloons. Falling gently downwards they caught air flows, eventually finding their way into eyes and nostrils, making it seem as though one was sniffing through feathers. This caused itching in sensitive membranes in the nose and throat until it drove hay-fever sufferers crazy. In those circumstances, the most vulnerable found it sheer torture – especially those who couldn't reach their noses. Once, last summer, an old gentleman with limited use of his arms, who lived next door to Maisie, cried all night saying that he was being driven out of his mind. He took a lot of calming until he received a relieving dose of anti-histamine from a visiting doctor, one of the few who make house calls in the area.

For the most part, summer brought a feeling of well-being and above all, flowers of all kinds that filled the garden, their fragrances wafting in through her open windows. This was Albert's territory. He had a special skill at making plants grow and it was through his efforts that the garden looked so spectacular. But then Albert was special, very special indeed and Maisie was proud of him.

Maisie's new apartment was just what she wanted. She left her youth long ago and knew that moving into these rooms, meant losing some of her already limited freedom, but she had to prepare for the onset of old age, however distant that might be. Better to do it now. Heaven knows she had faced enough hardship in her life.

She never regretted coming here, besides if she had not she would never have got to know Albert. Her other companions were good

133

sorts, but Albert was the one who had made her life so special. It was, without a doubt, the happiest she had ever been in her life. Albert helped her to put aside all her fears and helplessness in the face of her situation and for her part, she held a mysterious power over him. He was truly her man.

Seeing the children playing nearby took her back to her own childhood. It was not particularly happy. Her father and mother had not really wanted her and she was made to feel a liability. She knew in her heart that she must have been difficult to look after, but that was no reason to not love her or treat her like any other child. Her parents, who were none too bright, didn't exactly encourage her siblings to behave badly, but nevertheless they did. They must have taken their cue from something or someone, because they never let up and the teasing and silly remarks cut into her soul and made her cry, but nobody seemed to care very much. Sometimes she would ask to be put to bed just to escape their torment, only to be told that she was ungrateful. Confused and trapped within her malfunctioning body, she led a terrible existence until her parents were visited by social services, tipped off by a neighbour after Maisie cut her wrists. Her excitable parents had run into the street in an alcoholic haze screaming murder. She was taken to hospital, the wound became infected and she nearly died of septicaemia. Her parents tried to cover up their bad behaviour, but when questioned by social workers, they readily admitted responsibility for bad parenting, quickly seeing the possibility of offloading Maisie.

Sure enough, she was fostered for a number of months by well-meaning people, before finally settling with a lady called Jean Pye, a well-known philanthropist and foster mother in Bristol. This changed her life.

Jean was the most caring of people who paid every attention to Maisie's needs, but was also clever enough to guide her carefully to grow up learning to face the world with all its challenges. It was from Jean that she learned that love did truly conquer all fear and uncertainty. Christmases, Easter celebrations, birthdays and so on, all became special events as they had never been before, for Maisie and the others, fostered by this wonderful person. Jean Pye enriched dozens of lives until she eventually died.

After that, Maisie was again alone. Although she mourned and missed her foster mother, her mentor and friend, she was aware that Jean had done a good job on her. So much so that she established herself well enough to know what she was entitled to and what she should demand as a right, but also with a gentle ability to influence and control others.

Getting to know Albert had been like being injected with pure sunshine. Albert had a similar childhood experience. His parents pretended to like him, but one night he overheard them arguing about what to do with him, each saying that he was preventing them from leading a normal life. Those hurtful remarks stained his mind and stayed with him forever, the voices playing over and over again in his bad dreams. He knew they were ashamed of him when they started to leave him outside on the patio when people came to call. It was a terrible way to treat your own son.

But Albert had also conquered his fears and turned into a remarkably talented man. He worked hard and ran a small gardening unit in a social enterprise and his plants were admired by many people for miles around. His greatest moment came many years ago, when Alan Thrower, TV gardening personality, visited his centre and presented him with a prize for successfully propagating plants in difficult conditions. Thrower was amazed at Albert's results and said he had green hands. Maisie knew that - she also knew that his hands had other talents.

She closed her eyes at the thought of Albert's hands and her head spun ever so slightly, as it did so, she smiled to herself. He had come along late in her life; but, so what. After all, it was never too late to enjoy new experiences. Maisie was grateful to be delivered from ignorance; grateful for new friendships; grateful for those hands. Those hands that had a grip of iron and yet a touch like a feather.

A knock at the door made her open her eyes.

"Yes," she said, "who is it please?"

A pleasant west-country accent answered.

"It's me, Kerry," said a young voice. "I thought I'd come and see how you were in all this heat. Can I help you with anything?"

Maisie smiled. After Jean Pye, the world was full of Kerrys, always concerned for and looking after other people. They had become good friends and over time Kerry came to know everything there was to know about Maisie, and Albert for that matter. Maisie knew people had concerns and made stupid judgements about the two of them, but not Kerry.

Maisie also knew all Kerry's secrets. At first she was quite shocked to learn she was a lesbian, even though she really didn't understand what it was all about. They talked, sometimes late into the night, about all sorts of things, and eventually it included Kerry's sexual proclivity. Then it all became a lot clearer. Maisie was inquisitive, in a childlike way, and Kerry accepted this with humour and good grace. Then one night, when Kerry felt particularly stressed after a bad day working with her loathsome manager, she called in on Maisie and produced a bottle of sweet sherry. With what few inhibitions remained, they talked and laughed, and spent hours giggling like school children as Kerry unveiled her life.

She had given a lot of thought to what she was going to tell Maisie when the time came, but as the alcohol flowed through her veins and the evening gathered pace, it was inevitable that she would spare nothing. Maisie sat open-eyed with a big grin on her face as Kerry went into the most intimate details of the fun she had in her life. As she did so, she laughed at Maisie's frequent punctuation of the conversation with, "Oh my, well really."

Most amusing of all was when Kerry showed Maisie her belly-button piercing. Maisie couldn't quite reach to touch it, but marvelled at the crystal setting. Then she was shocked when Kerry stuck out her tongue and revealed a silver stud.

"Oh my, well really?" said Maisie, predictably.

Kerry laughed again. "How did I know you were going to say that?"

"But doesn't it affect your taste buds?" said Maisie with a frown.

"No, not at all. It makes for an interesting snog though."

Maisie slowly reached up to her mouth with her forearm and she just couldn't stop chuckling. Kerry joined in and despite the decade's difference in their ages, they laughed like two teenage girls at a sleepover.

They had been firm friends for five years now and their friendship had gone from strength to strength. Maisie not only enjoyed what she called 'the naughty bits' of their conversation, but most of all it was the way that she was effortlessly included in all sorts of highs and lows in Kerry's life, so much so that she knew her like a sister. She was trusted, asked her views and shared privileged information. Having a friend, a girl, to share all manner of things with, not just the intimate matters, was a joy.

"You're deep in thought today, Maisie, what's up?" said Kerry.

"Oh, nothing, just reflecting on how nice it is to look up and see you when you pop in and check on me from time to time. I suppose it's because I appreciate how you have brought so many new things to my life. The trouble is my dear, I don't think the deal has been that equal."

Kerry frowned and got down on one knee and held two of Maisie's fingers. "Now then, listen to me. Without you to tell me off for taking drugs I might not be here now. So don't give me that, my love."

Maisie smiled and gazed out of the window. Of course, Kerry was correct, but it wasn't just her drug habit that she had been instrumental in sorting out; there was something else she had arranged, in a subtle kind of way.

Across at the far end of the garden Albert was dead-heading some of the early roses in preparation for the show of buds. Kerry stood up and moved behind Maisie, putting her hands on her shoulders and gently massaging the joints as she watched her look at him. She touched her neck softly, felt the quickening pulse and bent down, whispering in her ear, "Maisie Campbell, you little devil!"

After twenty minutes watching Albert, Maisie was fast asleep. Her mind was somewhere pleasant and this was reflected by a peaceful smile on her face. Kerry gently stroked her head and then tiptoed out of the room.

Kerry went out into the garden and caught Albert's eye. He smiled back at her and gave her a wave.

"How are you Albert," she shouted. "Keeping well I hope?"

"Fair to middling, Kerry. How's herself?" he replied in a stuttering voice, nodding towards the French windows ten metres away.

"Now how do you think she is? She missed you of course."

Albert smiled. He liked to be missed. Being missed by someone was worth so much. All the accolades on his gardening prowess and other good things in his life paled into insignificance in comparison to that.

He pointed to his legs.

"Running repairs, that's all, running repairs." He straightened up and stretched his arms above his head. He was a tall muscular man and towered over Kerry. He looked directly at her.

"Shall I wash my hands then?" he said, like a schoolboy seeking permission from his mother.

"Yes, do that, and give her about thirty more minutes before you pop in and see her, she's tired out, but mostly from ogling you I think," she laughed out loud, adding, "you lucky feller."

He smiled broadly back at her. Albert didn't mind the teasing. In any case, it would take him an age to load the wheelbarrow and tidy up. It was an awkward process these days and he had fallen down the week before, hence the need for 'running repairs'. He made his way to the large green garden shed and effortlessly unloaded his heavy gardening gear. His strong arms and hands made light work of the heavy spades, forks and pick-axes and he effortlessly laid them on shelves above waist height so they would be more accessible to him the next morning. Too much clutter under his feet was dangerous, it was too easy for him to fall over – if he did, then it would take him a devil of a time to get back up again.

When he was finished with the heavy chores, he went to the greenhouse at the side of the large shed and peered in at the seedlings that had long since grown into young plants and were ready for planting out. He couldn't resist walking up and down the wide aisles. Smiling to himself, he reached out and gently touched the soft, flimsy petals of all plants that he had nurtured as though he was their father.

For a powerfully built man he had surprisingly gentle hands. But then that's what Alan Thrower had said, five years ago, "Albert, your hands are absolute magic, I think you have special powers in those mitts, so make sure you take care of them."

Albert was in thrall to him and for days afterwards would wash his hands and sit looking at them during the evening. After that he concentrated hard on the plants he was nurturing and to his enormous surprise and delight they flourished even more. He grew the biggest and best roses, his Clematis were the toast of the town and people came from miles around to buy his bedding plants. Thrower must have been right.

It was during this period of success that he got to know Maisie. Kerry introduced them. She had done so by creating opportunities for them to meet, sensitively dealing with Albert's shyness with a twinkle in her eye and careful planning. Later, she gently schooled them both in the art of getting to know each other. Eventually, they hit it off and discovered that their backgrounds were so similar. After that they just seemed to talk for ages, liking and understanding each other and discovering more and more as time went on. It was as though there wasn't enough time left in the world for them to say all there was to say to each other.

They formed a strong bond from that moment on and he would do absolutely anything to make life comfortable and happy for Maisie. He was totally besotted by her.

The only threat to their relationship came from Mr and Mrs MaGuire, people who should have known better in their position, but they thought it appropriate to object to their close friendship and made their lives a misery. What did they know? How could they be so cruel?

It was the MaGuires who started to make life bad for Maisie and he couldn't stand that; it made him angry – very angry. He couldn't help himself. It was impossible for him to stand back and let that happen, not after the awful lives they had been forced to live.

Albert tried hard to reason with them. Because of their position it was important to keep on their right side, but they were power crazy, typical of small-minded people in positions where control over others can be easily exercised. They weren't the type to listen. In the end, he grew to hate them even more than he had his parents. But things were different now. He had given a great deal of careful thought about the situation and knew that his life and Maisie's happiness was in his own hands.

The MaGuires soon learned that too.

At about five p.m. Albert washed his face and hands, especially his hands, put on a clean shirt and went to see Kerry. It wasn't far to her office, but it took him some time to negotiate his way there. But he didn't mind. When she saw him coming towards her she smiled and raised her finger to the left side of her head at eye-level looking quizzically, half-teasing, upwards. Then as if in recognition of something suddenly remembered, she pulled an, "Aha!" kind of face and pursed her lips, before disappearing into her office. She always did this and Albert laughed at her. It was all part of a kind of "...I know where you're going..." ritual between them.

Kerry came out of her office with a medium sized plastic tub of cream and handed it to Albert. He took the top off and put it to his nose. It smelled of sweet freesias and made him close his eyes. She smiled at this, knew what it was destined for and was pleased about her part in it all - the cupid instigator, the encourager and the provider. As far as she was concerned, this was the part of her new job that she most enjoyed – the ability to do those little things that made people's lives so much better. Before her promotion she had been an assistant with little influence or power and now things had changed. Now she could really make a difference.

Albert screwed the top back on the tub, thanked her, then turned and made his way as quickly as he could to Maisie's apartment. When he reached her room, he knocked on the door like a nervous schoolboy.

"Come in," said Maisie. "I know it's you, Albert, I've been waiting for you."

Albert went in and saw her lying under a sheet on a large framed bed. Unabashed, he went over to the bed, leaned awkwardly over and pecked her on the cheek. She had such power over him, it felt as though he was walking into a magnetic field, a beautiful one full of lights and colours that made his heart beat and his head swirl. He felt that he could stride over mountains or fight lions – all for Maisie. He was completely under her spell.

"I missed you," she said fondly. "Where have you been?"

"Running repairs, just running repairs, my dear," he replied, gently unscrewing the top on the white tub of cream. The scent escaped and filled the room almost immediately.

140

"Oh, that's a lovely smell," said Maisie.

"Your usual, ma'am?" Albert asked, and without waiting for an answer he leaned forward straight-legged and gently turned her to one side whilst holding the sheet delicately so that it didn't fall away from her body.

"You don't need to worry about that, Albert," she protested. "I'm not shy of you, my love."

He touched her lightly on the side of the head and said nothing. Then he put his right hand into the cream, letting it lightly coat his fingers and gently rubbed it into her shoulders and neck. Maisie was in seventh heaven. It is difficult to describe the true value of touch to anyone who had spent years without gentle physical contact of this kind. Maisie did not regard it as she would a clinical bed-bath or physiotherapy, it was nice, truly nice. It was Albert's hands that did the trick - his special hands.

Maisie breathed slowly and began to feel quite warm. As Albert wove his magic, she looked up and said, "I spoke to Kerry today and she seemed happy enough, organising everyone and everything. Do you think she's enjoying her new job?"

Albert looked up and grinned.

"Yes, she is, very much. You can see it every day. She's very popular and works hard for everybody. Nothing is ever too much trouble."

He looked up blankly at the ceiling and his massaging slowed as he added, "She's so much better than the MaGuires."

"You can say that again," said Maisie. "They have gone haven't they – tell me they have? I do so hope that they don't ever come back. Tell me that they won't, Albert."

She let out a sigh and moved her body against the gentle rub of his hands.

Albert slowed his massage and his eyes, unseen by Maisie, narrowed. "Maisie, if you don't stop asking stupid questions I'll tell my special hands to stop work."

She playfully protested, then said no more. That suited him and he continued to work slowly down her back, following the exaggerated left to right twisted S-shape of her spinal column that blighted her life. His massage along the vertebrae eased the increasingly painful arthritis she felt these days. Albert gently worked the cream into her shoulders and back, humming as he did so.

Maisie wriggled with anticipation under his soft touch as he extended his massage and felt a familiar watery sensation in her stomach as he worked his way along her painfully thin thighs. He finished after about twenty minutes and by then she had drifted off to sleep.

Albert wrapped her gently in the large blue blanket that had been placed at the bottom of the bed, then awkwardly leaned forward and kissed her. He had to move a large hoist to one side to be able to do so. Straightening up, he stood for a few moments just looking at her and raised his hands, palms upwards. The power to make flowers grow and to do this too. All this joy had come so much later in life after so much unhappiness in his youth. Tears came to his eyes with the sure knowledge that he could make someone feel so very good, especially someone as nice as Maisie.

He moved quietly away from her bed, where she was now fast asleep and purring like a kitten. As he did so he hit his leg against the hoist and there was a loud clang of metal and he stopped and stood absolutely still hoping not to have woken her. Satisfied he hadn't done any damage, he left the room, leaving a soft blue safety light on, and walked down the corridor, his callipers clunking with each stride.

The next day was again bright and sunny. Maisie woke up smiling and happy. After she had been helped to wash and clean her teeth, she was dressed and placed in her electric wheelchair. She went through the usual tests to make sure that two useful fingers on each hand were working so that she could use the controls properly. Up until a few years ago three fingers worked well, but not now. Then her carer adjusted her headrest so that her weak neck was supported to one side of the large hump on her shoulder.

She gripped the small control lever, moving it to the right and the chair glided effortlessly and carefully out through the French windows and onto the patio. When she was outside, she called out to people on the other patios to the left and right of her - her 'palsied pals' as she called them. She looked up from under a sun-shade hat that she wore to protect her eyes, being unable to raise her arms to shade her face and looked further into the garden. Albert was putting compost on the roses and she raised her left arm, barely six inches, as far as it would effectively go, and waved to him. Kerry stood next to him and pointed in Maisie's direction. He straightened up and as he did so nearly fell over his callipers, stumbling forward in several loping steps before regaining his footing. His laughter was so raucous and loud Maisie could hear him from twenty metres away and he waved wildly at her with both arms.

"Careful, Albert, we don't want you having more running repairs," she thought to herself.

Kerry looked at them both and smiled at the way they gazed at each other, then decided to walk the long way back to her office in the warden's block. She wanted to take a look at the windows to the rear of the sheltered accommodation that needed urgent repair. The place was finally being brought back to a good state of repair after many years of being neglected during the poor wardenship of Reginald MaGuire and his odious wife Gwendolyn. Just thinking of the names brought their images to mind and she shivered. He and his wife had been the nastiest people she had ever had the misfortune to work for. But they were gone now. Gone but not forgotten, even by the local detective who investigated their sudden disappearance without a trace. He gave up returning to the warden's cottage to look for clues and Kerry was glad of that, because it meant that she had been able to move into the tied accommodation and make it her own home. To top this good luck, she also got the job as warden of the residential home.

As she mused about the recent goings on, she passed several of Albert's compost heaps and, as she had done from the day she had been appointed manager, she put her fingers to her nose. The largest heap always seemed incredibly smelly, with a particularly pungent odour. She wasn't sure what he was rotting down, but whatever it was, it produced brilliant roses.

Whilst Kerry disappeared into her office, Maisie and Albert continued to gaze at each other over the lawn and beautiful flowered borders for a little longer and then he gently raised his hands and wiggled them in the air.

Albert's hands were, indeed, very special to both their lives.

# Work With Me

Preparing was bad enough, but not as bad as getting my mind right to deal with the rows of faces in front me, some leaning awkwardly in their seats absentmindedly cleaning spectacles, others reading the papers and ready to wave them at me, in extremis to loudly over-talk me. Order. Order. That is all I want. Order - to make my best pitch. To inform. To be valued and listened to. To feel that I have made a difference, whether or not it is at first recognised by the faces opposite.

I am new to all this. How do I look? Do I wear make-up, or not? It doesn't do to get sensitive, there is no room or leeway for that – the audience is merciless. One slip or any sign of weakness and they will pounce. But they are not all so vacuous – some respond well and take what I say despite the difference in position between us. Is this public duty or personal ego? Then I reflect: No, it is almost joyful and worth all the hard work. I love it and t gives me a glow. It sustains me and leads me to want to do all this again. It is why I am here. It is worth the long haul to get to where I stand this day – looking at the faces.

Today is different. They want to listen. What price politics: of envy, of difference, of ability, or simply, of indifference, but above all, to follow the corporate message, no matter what I may think. It does not sit easily sometimes but I do what I must out of loyalty and discipline. I look to the left where the moderator sits, ready to restore *order* if the atmosphere should become ill-disciplined. Otherwise it is me on show, me to present and be judged on my delivery; my script, my ability to be persuasive.

My Nemesis rises with a question. It is deliberately simple and yet incisive, designed to show that it is being asked because the message has not gotten through clearly enough. I respond, carefully, quietly and persuasively; no rancour, and no sign of exasperation at the failure of the questioner to understand basic principles. Just resignation and they sit again. More questions follow, but this time from supporters who aim to show they understood and they do want to know more. My heart leaps at a rare thank you for the clarity of my explanation – yesterday, ill-discipline, shouting and tension; today, civilised behaviour. Such is life.

My spell on my feet ends. It was a success. The moderator rises – having not had to shout *order* is a welcome relief to him and to me. He will note the quality of my work and overlook the two boys exchanging football cards out of my sight at the back of the class. He will make me feel high or miserable, and a lot depends on the faces opposite. They grin at me. They know the importance of observations. They have unreasonable power to affect the outcome. They are not stupid. Perhaps the system is.

But whatever happens, I want to enjoy teaching and will drive my will to succeed in getting knowledge across to my charges, despite the challenges and the politics.

It is my destiny.

# GOLLUM

Frances Bellerby tidied the living room of her spacious detached home on the edge of the New Forest for the second time that day. In her mid forties and retired from a career in insurance she was now settled as a housewife with two teenage children at boarding school. Being pleased with her life and her home was a sign of her character; everything in line, just right and under control. She kept a tight rein on things, it was her style - no fuss, just the certain knowledge of what was right and how things should be.

Her husband Phillip was, however, a constant source of confusion to her. He was a successful property developer, but to her consternation he didn't think like her and often saw the world from a totally different perspective. Any sign of attempted control – something that was hard-wired into Frances's character – and his heels dug firmly into the ground. It wasn't a big deal at all and from what her friends told her about their spouses, all men were the same. They sometimes behaved like posturing peacocks, oiling cricket bats that they would probably never use again and pulling their tummies in when passing a blonde on the beach, or in Phillip's case, joining the freemasons with its fraternal values and strange rituals. On the other hand, they ran companies, built bridges and aimed at the moon. She smiled at the thought that, whatever their profession or position in life, they were subject to the playful and superficial. It was a damned good job they all had women to look after them. She laughed to herself and fluffed up the cushions on the tapestry-covered sofa.

Frances was happy. She and Phillip were still in love and her man had ever let her down. He was a lovely chap who just needed to be controlled – like all men – and she tried to oblige.

Dealing with dust that the cleaner failed to spot that morning annoyed her, and she removed a small piece of fluff from a shelf and wiped the duster across an adjacent already clean rail 'just to be sure'.

Despite Phillip's requests for her not to tidy his study, Frances found it irritating to see dust accumulating and went in to give it just a 'flick'. It really had to be done. He was silly anyway, he had no secrets and neither did she.

As she moved the yellow duster across his bookshelf something dropped onto the floor. It was a photograph, slightly grainy and sepia rather than clear black and white. She remembered that Phillip had shown it to her some years ago. It was of a human skull, placed in a small alcove at about head height and to the left of an archway in a cellar wall. The stonework was old and worn in parts. Above the archway the words, "*Know Thyself*," were inscribed on a large keystone.

It was all part of his initiation as a freemason when he had been in the Netherlands and it meant something to him. He had been told to sit and contemplate the words of advice, which were to be central to his attitude and way of life.

"What tosh!" she thought. But if it suited him, then so be it. Who doesn't know themselves anyway? Silly man. Why ask, and what was it all for? To Frances, it was positive proof as to why God put women on the earth, which was to make up for men's meandering minds and need for direction.

Frances certainly knew herself. She knew what she could do and what she couldn't and the difference between right and wrong, there was absolutely no question about that.

She prepared a neat tray of Earl Grey tea and Rich Tea biscuits, nibbling at one and leaving two, then settled back to read a magazine and listen to Woman's Hour on the radio. But she soon got irritated with women on the programme taking about 'low self esteem', or the value of counselling for this or that. Frances, or, "St Frances", as Phillip called her when she was on her high horse, found it difficult to suffer other people's problems. Let him joke, she thought, it mattered not a jot. In her world there was only black and white – no grey whatsoever. That suited her.

She switched the radio off and stood up, stretching as she did so, catching sight of herself in the large mirror over the fireplace. It was pleasing to look younger than her years and she slowly ran her hands down her sides. For a fleeting second she wished that Phillip could be home with her today, it would be so good if he worked part time.

Just then, Toby, the family spaniel, rushed up to her, tail wagging, and sat down on her foot with his back to her, looking up, imploring her to take him out.

"Toby, you nuisance you know I never take you out before lunch. Oh, heck, who cares?" she said, reluctantly submitting to a break in her routine. He knew he had won the encounter and barked at her.

She gathered up her car and house keys and soon Toby was tethered by the lead and pulling hard towards the door. Normally, she would head for the coast because she liked walking along the beach. But today she chose to head for the New Forest, to drive along the A35 then turn into the Rhinefield area, with its ancient gnarled trees and masses of rhododendron bushes that thrived on the peat-rich soil. She parked in a car park, near the public toilets and ice cream van that was doing a brisk trade with excited children chirping as they waited in a small queue.

It was a warm, sultry June day and she didn't need a coat so she left it in the car. Toby was allowed to run off into the woodland with Frances following. The sunlight picked out the colours of the trees and the profusion of purple, red and yellow rhododendrons, many of which had grown to over eighteen feet high and equally as wide. It was a magnificent sight.

Frances day-dreamed for a while, but all of a sudden, she realised that Toby was out of sight. Annoyed, she called his name but there was no response and moved into a thick, untracked area of the forest to look for him. He was normally a good dog and she was certain she would find him. She thought she heard barking ahead, but couldn't be sure. This encouraged her to follow the sound and go deeper into the thick bushes and trees. As she did so, it got darker, swarm of midges flew into her face and she flapped her hands to remove them. Some sharp branches scratched her skin and for a moment she became entangled in the undergrowth. When she turned around, the path seemed to be just as difficult to return through, so reluctantly she pushed on, cursing Toby and determined to put him straight on the lead as soon as she found him. She continued for a few minutes then noticed a bright clearing visible through the mesh of bushes, creepers and trees, and headed straight for it.

At last she burst through the bushes into a clearing and immediately set about swotting midges from her face and hair. When she finished, she called for Toby again, but there was no sound. She didn't swear often, but today she cursed his hide.

Pausing for a moment to get her bearings she became aware of the silence. She knew that she must have walked a long way from the main tourist paths through the forest. The clearing was about twenty-five metres square and the grass in the middle was a lush light green because it enjoyed direct sunlight through the gap in the trees above. It was quite beautiful, ringed by rhododendron bushes and woodland. Despite the absence of Toby, which was mildly worrying, it was a pleasant place to stand and gather her wits. She looked around and took in the scenery. There were old tree stumps and logs to the left and small thorn bushes behind and to her front, with what looked like a path leading out and she resolved to follow that to find her dog. Then to her right she saw what looked like rocks and slabs of concrete and in the middle of it was a dark gap about eight inches high and six feet wide with a steel plate on top. Something made her stare straight at it. She noticed that the lid was padlocked to the edge of a metal frame around the dark gap in the concrete.

Then she froze and recoiled with fear. Out of the gap came a hand. She put her fingers to her mouth and caught her breath. Someone was inside the concrete and metal in front of her. But how did they get there?

"Help me," said a weak voice, unmistakably female. "Help, you've got to help me, please?"

Frances walked slowly towards the concrete slabs and looked into the dark gap.

"Hello, yes, can I help? Who are you? I am Frances Bellerby, who are you?"

She reached for her mobile telephone, but harrumphed when she realised it was in her jacket which she had chosen not to wear because it was so warm.

"You must help me, please get me out of here?" said the imprisoned woman. Frances saw that the metal lid was in effect the door to the hole in which the woman was imprisoned.

"I will, I will, but I need to know who you are and get help. I can't break that large padlock," she said. "I must go and get someone to release you."

"No, no, no…please don't go."

By now the woman was sobbing.

Frances was confused. "You mustn't worry, I don't understand, surely you want to be free don't you?"

"Yes, yes," said the woman. "But please stay for just a few more moments, please?"

Frances frowned and reached towards the woman who took her hands and held them very tightly - too tightly.

"Oh, dear, don't hold my hands so hard, you'll cut off the circulation," she said trying to be calming and jokey. But as she tried to pull away she became aware that the woman was holding on to her like a limpet. The woman's eyes were full of tears and yet she seemed to stare over Frances's left shoulder.

Frances half turned to see what the woman was looking at, moving awkwardly because she was still gripped tightly and gulped in shock and surprise.

Standing over her was a character that resembled Gollum from the story The Lord of the Rings. He had a bone-thin body and wore loose fitting blue pyjama-style clothes with a leather belt. He hardly resembled a normal human being, with a head that was triangular shaped, almost bald and with two of the most protruding eyes she had ever seen in her life.

As she looked back at the woman in the bunker, she felt a thud to her skull and tasted blood in her mouth. Her head filled with bright lights and loud ringing and she passed out.

Frances wasn't sure how long she had been unconscious, but as her vision returned all she could see was a letterbox shaped area of light in front of and four feet above the ground. She saw vague shapes through the lighted area. Her heart froze when she realised what had happened - she was in the hole and the other woman was now outside it.

Sitting up and despite the pain in her head she scrambled to the gap and looked out. To her horror, she saw a dishevelled woman kneeling in front of the man, who looked even more repulsive than on first sight. He smiled at the woman, and stood over her, his arms folded, looking nonchalantly up at the forest canopy. He appeared to be enjoying the power he had over her. She was crying and begging him to let her go. After a short pause, he pointed to the path, indicating with a dismissive wave of his hand that she should take it. Surprised and yet noticeably grateful the woman seemed to thank him, which only made him turn away looking upwards again, with a kind of childish expression of nonchalant disinterest.

The woman needed no further encouragement and stood up, shakily stumbling towards the path back into the forest. Seconds after she disappeared into the gloom, the man turned slowly and looked straight at Frances. She was petrified. As he gazed at her he giggled like a child and put his fingers to his mouth. He crouched forward, picked up what looked like a large club and turned sharply, scampering through the gap in the trees in hot pursuit of the woman.

She nearly hyperventilated at the thought of being left alone in the cold dark bunker and desperately shouted after him.

"No, no, please don't go. I must be let out. This is stupid. No don't go, please."

She screamed at him, imploring him to come back and let her out, and fell backwards onto her bottom against a rough concrete wall behind her, hurting her side. What was happening to her? As she sat there she felt a rough straw mattress to her left and a couple of blankets. This was a prison and she was in it.

To her horror, she heard a woman's piercing scream twice, then a dog yelping, then nothing. Fearing the worst, she fainted.

When Frances awoke she was frightened and shivering with the cool of the night. Despite her fear, she tried to understand what had happened to her. Why had the woman held her so tightly? Then without warning she had been hit by the Gollum-like person. He was so ugly. Just recalling his face frightened her. He looked old, with protruding eyes and pallid and slightly wrinkled skin.

Her throat was dry and her head ached. But somehow she had to keep her wits about her. Slowly she felt her way around her prison. To her rear was a concrete wall and to her immediate right was another wall slightly damaged and jagged with stones out of place and holes through which earth had fallen. In front of her was a similarly misshapen concrete wall but with the gap immediately above it. She moved down a slight slope to the left for about six metres, which indicated that the concrete construction had sunk awkwardly into the ground at an angle. It was also obvious that this part had been used as a make-shift toilet area and her nose wrinkled. She made her way back to the gap and was thankful that the stench seemed to stay where it was, probably because the air was being drawn through the bunker and out in another direction.

In the middle of the blankets there were several plastic bottles, but only one had any liquid in. After opening and smelling the contents she thought it was safe to drink and tipped the warm liquid over her tongue and into her throat. It was stale water, but was at least liquid. Tears welled in her eyes and she wondered what Phillip was doing. He must be worried and would have called the police. Thinking about the yelp she heard from a dog upset her and she gripped her hands tightly at the thought that he might have been hurt, or worse. She put her head down on the sticky, prickly straw mattress, pulled a smelly blanket over her body, eventually falling into a cold and uncomfortable asleep.

The morning sun filtered through the gaps in the trees and warmed the metal lid to the bunker and Frances's body responded by shivering less. Warmer, she fell into a deeper sleep for an hour or so, finally waking with a start, wondering where she was. She banged her head as she tried to stand up and had to sit down again abruptly. When her head cleared and stopped throbbing, she became aware of trees rustling and birds singing, otherwise it was very quiet.

Frances fought hard to control her emotions and several times was on the verge of sheer panic at being incarcerated in such a small space. Yoga techniques helped her to regain composure and as she was concentrating hard, she heard footsteps on the gritty earth coming towards the bunker and her heart leapt. When she reached the gap, she was disappointed, her spirits fell when she saw the man's odd face peering in at her. He smiled maniacally and held a brown paper sack in her direction. She instinctively reached for it, but as she did so he withdrew it and pulled a childlike face, screwed up, that implied, *"naughty, naughty, don't grab!"* He seemed to enjoy exercising power in the same way that a child teases a puppy.

"Please," she said. "I'm thirsty. I know that you must be a really nice man, so let me have something to drink, please?"

This seemed to do the trick and he magnanimously threw the sack through the gap, and sat watching her as she opened it. On seeing two water bottles, she opened one and drained it completely. The liquid re-hydrated her body as she swallowed it in big gulps. Despite her hunger she chose to only nibble at the sandwiches. His face looking down at her made her lose her appetite. To her delight he had included several tubes of fruit pastels and she knew that the sugar would do her good. She would eat the sandwiches later and save some of the pastels.

Looking out of the gap, she pleaded, "Look. I don't know why you are doing this, but I want to help, really I do. Please let me out and we can talk?"

The man's face screwed up and he half-smiled, almost sarcastically, insolently, as though he had heard that line many times before.

"I look after youse, not youse look after meese," he said in a strange tone of voice and folded his arms again, turning away from her.

Frances felt bile rise in her throat and she tried hard to restrain her anger and appear conciliatory.

"Please don't say that. I can help you, I really can. I used to help people like you," she stumbled over the words, realising as he jumped up, that her work with people who are mentally ill might not impress - she was right. It seemed to touch a raw nerve.

"Youse looked after by me. Meese locking youse up, not you locking meese up. See, see…" he screamed at her and pointed a gnarled finger in her direction. He was now agitated, his face contorted and red.

Then she lost control. "But I don't know you, I haven't harmed you. Why are you doing this? You will be caught you know, you really will, then you will be punished."

She was aware that she was shouting at him and it was having a bad effect, but she could not help it. His face was now draining colour and he moved backwards slowly. Then he just turned and ran. Frances cursed her momentary lack of control.

"Come back, now, you bastard, you creep. Let me out of here, for pity's sake, let me out?" She screamed at him in vain as he disappeared into the forest without looking back.

Falling back against the wall, tears welled up again, not out of weakness, but frustration. Phillip must be worried sick about her whereabouts and safety. Her situation was so awful that she hated the man enough to kill him – this was something that she had never experienced in her life before. Anger, despair and helplessness.

Discipline had to be the order of the day and she knew it would be her only solace. It was important to develop a routine and she began by tidying her prison by moving rocks, plastic bottles and other rubbish down the slope. She inspected every inch of the immediate area, mentally cataloguing every part of her environment. Several parts in the brickwork might yield, because there were small gaps where the mortar had degraded, but they would all need some work and without an instrument this would be near impossible. After a while she decided to reach outside the gap and feel around the metal lid for a handle or some idea as to what held the metal lid to the concrete. Soon she located a large padlock linked through two metal rings, but rattling it hard soon confirmed that it was securely locked and fastened. No amount of shaking would break it loose and the metal rings were too solid to give way. She fell back exhausted and decided to chew some pastels for energy.

"Why is this happening to me?" she said out loud, her nose fizzing and eyes moist. "Why bloody me?"

The afternoon wore on and the heat inside the bunker made her thirsty and although she knew she had to conserve the water she drank it all. By early evening she had no more provisions except half a roll of pastels. Then it got dark and she settled down for another chilly night.

Surprisingly, Frances slept soundly, mentally and physically exhausted from her exertions. The following morning she awoke as the sun warmed the metal lid, sat up and rubbed her eyes and neatly folded the filthy blankets. Next, she did some strenuous stretches to keep her body strong and supple, and mind alert, before chewing the two remaining fruit pastels. The sugar-stream flowed through her body like a charge of electricity. Closing her eyes, she sat back against the rough concrete wall and planned a dinner party for twelve guests in the utmost detail: starter, sorbet, main course and dessert, with the very finest wines. This mental agility kept her calm and in typical Frances fashion she argued with herself about the selection for the cheese-board.

She had just finished identifying the ingredients to make petite fours to go with the Kenyan pea-berry coffee and imagined the choice of background music, when there was shatteringly loud bang. More crashes rained down as someone banged something hard repeatedly on the metal lid. Her ears rang and she covered them with her hands. After about two minutes noise stopped as abruptly as it began. The silence felt heavy. Her head buzzed so much it hurt.

Staggering to the gap she looked out. It was the man. He sat there, arms folded, looking at the sky with a nonchalant expression on his face. He had a paper bag at his side and the sight of it made Frances's saliva flow; she was desperate for a drink of water. She knew she had to pander to him and braced herself.

"Good morning," she said, trying her utmost to appear unruffled. "Look, I am really sorry I upset you yesterday. There was no need for that."

He looked at her, sneered and raised a paper sack.

"Please, I am so thirsty," she said, saliva thick in her mouth.

Holding the sack a few inches from her outstretched arm with one hand, he beckoned her with the other.

Tilting his head to one side he said, "Blouses, youse blouses..." Then he put his hand to his mouth and giggled.

Frances blanched and held back a scream of frustration.

"What?"

Her heart sank and she was horrified. "My blouse, you want my bloody blouse?"

He nodded, holding his body as if he was trying to suppress fits of the giggles.

Frances felt enormous rage in the face of her powerlessness and humiliation, and it spread through her body like a drink of ice-cold water. She closed her eyes. He was a creep, a bloody pervert, but she was helpless and needed water, so had no choice. With her eyes still shut she imagined she was in her bedroom at home, undid the buttons and slipped the cotton blouse off her shoulders. Looking up she saw his repulsive face leering at her and it made her feel sick. But she would do anything to get some water.

Reluctantly, Frances held the blouse at the gap of the bunker. But before she could reach out, he quickly grabbed it, and pulled the sack away from her outstretched hand saying, "brassises, now brassises!"

"Oh, God," she said quietly through gritted teeth. "You bastard."

She held his ridiculous gaze for a moment, and resigned to her situation, unclipped unclip her brassiere. This time she glared at him, full of hate and disgust. As she watched him, she noticed his face change and he actually looked scared. She held the brassiere close to her body with one hand and held out the other.

"The paper sack, first," she barked.

He shook his head violently.

"Yes, this stays on me, unless you give it to me," she said revealing a little more flesh as she let it hang looser. She wanted that paper sack and would do anything to get it and get out of the bunker.

A moment later he slowly moved the sack closer to her and she reached for it. He indicated that he wanted the brassiere and without thinking she held it out towards him with her other hand. Then in a swipe he grabbed the brassiere and pulled it out of her grasp, at the same time maintaining a grip on the paper sack full of bottled water and food. She shrieked in surprise and anger.

Happy with this success he danced around waving the brassiere in the air, laughing maniacally and kicked the paper sack so that it burst open. It was frightening to see someone acting in such a manic way. The contents flew everywhere. He danced and pointed at her, enjoying her vulnerability and taunted her.

All of a sudden he froze and stood staring at her.

There was something strange about the look in his eyes. Frances realised that he was transfixed at the sight of her breasts. She seized the initiative.

"I need water to drink. Look, you can touch me if you give me water. I need water," she repeated, pushing her chest slightly forward.

The man walked slowly towards her and almost without looking at it, picked up a bottle of mineral water and sat in front of the bunker just looking at her. He didn't move at all for a few minutes. She knew she had to be patient this time.

"Water, please, water," she said softly.

He moved a little closer and as he did so Frances noticed a key hanging on the right side of his belt. Her mind worked quickly.

"Here, give me water and you can touch me. Would you like that?"

The words almost choked in her throat.

His breathing quickened and he moved closer, his eyes transfixed by her breasts, as he unscrewed the top of the bottle and offered it to her through the gap. She didn't take hold of it, because she wanted his right hand to be employed holding the plastic container. He put the bottle to her mouth and she reached through with both hands, her left steadying his right hand holding the bottle, and her right reaching slowly outwards to his belt and towards the key that hung from it. She sipped the cool liquid whilst at the same time holding his hand tightly with her left. Her other hand moved along his belt, feeling for the metal shape of the key. She found it and tried to carefully remove it, but it was difficult to get off the clasp without him noticing. Despite this, she was making good progress and several times it almost came loose.

The water was getting lower so she pretended to take large gulps whilst only swallowing a small amount - the key was loosening, but not enough. Inevitably, the water ran out and as he was about to withdraw the empty bottle she accidentally knocked it to the floor. There was nothing else she could do and she pulled his hand towards her, placing it squarely on her breast. To her alarm, far from fumbling with her, which, although unpleasant, would have given more time, he screamed and jumped backwards as though he had

158

received a thousand volts of electricity. He had touched her but this was not what he really wanted. He was visibly scared out of his wits.

As he fell, he became aware of her right hand on his belt and reacted like a startled animal. She held on to the key for all she was worth and he tried to escape her grasp, screaming and almost out of his mind, smacking her arm repeatedly with his bony hands. The pain in her two fingers holding the key was excruciating, but she held on tight, her flesh scraping against the rough concrete edge.

"You bloody cretin, let me have the key, let me have it now," she screamed.

But the weight of his body, frail though it was, was greater than her fingers to cope with and he eventually broke free. He stood in front of the bunker and howled like a beaten dog, holding his head with both hands, swaying backwards and forwards. Then he turned and slowly shambled away unsteadily.

"Don't go, no don't go. I want the key and I want it now. Give it to me you bastard, give it to me."

But he left her, without a backward glance, as though she didn't exist.

Frances slid to the dirt floor, exhausted, badly scratched by the edge of the concrete bunker, her fingers sore and aching. She was too empty to cry, at last she had had enough, and felt completely beaten. It was clear to her that she would have even given sex to him to gain her freedom. Now he was gone and she might not even see him again. Her plan had failed. She felt a sense of utter dejection like never before.

Frances was strong-minded enough to know that she had to come out of this state of torpor and regain control of herself and dragged herself back to the gap. She was able to just about reach a packet of sweets that lay nearby, which she scooped towards her, but the remainder of the water and food stayed tantalisingly out of reach. That night she slept, despite shivering because of the lack of top clothing, very hungry and thirsty.

The next day saw no sign of her jailer and she began to believe that he would never come back and she would starve to death.

As the day drew on she despaired.

Waking from a doze, she thought that she heard a sound. Then it became clearer. It was a woman's voice, accompanied by faint steps coming across the gravel path.

"Buster, Buster. Damned dog. Buster, where are you? Come on you dumb dog, where are you?"

Frances was weak, but jumped quickly to the gap and could have fainted with delight as she saw a young woman of about thirty-five years walking towards the bunker. To her despair, she began to move in the opposite direction.

Her voice worked almost without her telling it to.

"Help, help, help, let me out of here," she shouted loudly.

The young woman stopped and looked around. Frances stuck both arms out of the gap and kept screaming whilst waving them around. The woman looked aghast and ran towards the bunker. When she got there she held Frances's hands.

"Oh, my God. What the hell is this?" she blurted. "Wait, I'll call the police."

Frances began to cry as the woman brought out a mobile telephone and said calmly, "Don't worry, I'll get you out of here, I promise."

Then, Frances froze. The man appeared behind the woman, with a large club. He smiled and looked straight at Frances. All of a sudden she felt totally impotent. If she warned the young woman and this chance contact failed, he would get angry and if he killed the woman Frances might never be free. On the other hand, she had replaced the other victim in the bunker, so would he do that again? Should she warn the woman or stay quiet and exchange places? Would Frances meet the same fate as her predecessor whose scream she had heard? What should she do? The seconds ticked by agonisingly and painfully, as though she was in a bad dream. She understood now the expression on the face of the woman she had found incarcerated three days ago. Now it was her dilemma.

The man crept up behind the woman and Frances's throat was so tight she was unable to form words of warning - all she could think of was her freedom. All she could do was look from him to the woman and then it was too late. He hit her hard and she fell to the floor with a thump and then stood smiling at the body.

Frances's heart was in her mouth as he reached for the key on his belt. Sure enough he unlocked the bunker lid and opened it, standing back holding the large club. It was difficult to resist the overwhelming urge to jump out and run like hell. But resist she did and her mind began to work properly. She decided to feign extreme frailty and crawled over the edge of the gap, making it seem that she could hardly move her muscles. He appeared to enjoy her helplessness and relaxed his stance, holding the club lower by his side.

Suddenly, he indicated in an agitated manner that the woman should be rolled into the bunker. This must have been what happened to Frances days earlier. He became irritated with her slowness as she pretended not to have any strength to move the woman's body. It was clear that he was not that strong himself and needed help. Now he got angry and danced around wildly, waving his arms, indicating that the manoeuvre had to be undertaken quickly.

"Of course it has to be done quickly, creepio, she may wake up in a minute and then it's two on to one!" thought Frances.

The man was now beginning to panic, because it didn't usually work out like this. The young woman began to moan and he went berserk. Jumping to the edge of the bunker he began pulling her towards him; she had to be incarcerated before she regained consciousness. He waved frantically at Frances urging her to push from the other side.

In a split second, she knew what to do and was glad she had kept herself supple. She sprang up, and as he gawped up at her in complete surprise, kicked him in the head and he fell backwards into the bunker. As he hit the ground she grabbed the edge of the metal lid and brought it down with a crash on his hand as he tried to climb out. He shrieked in pain. Sitting on the lid, holding it fast under her weight, she felt total relief and tears rolled down her dirty face. He was trapped.

After a while the woman regained consciousness and was horrified at the sight of Frances's tear streaked face and half-naked body, with the man screaming like a banshee in the bunker, unable to move the metal lid. It only took moments to explain the situation and the woman used her mobile to summon help.

161

The police arrived and Frances, now dressed in her blouse retrieved from the undergrowth, hugged the young woman tightly. It was all over.

She was safe.

Back home, warm and secure, Frances held onto her husband tightly and swore that she would never let him go. They cried buckets of tears as despair was replaced by joy, but they were both still in a state of shock at the thought of what could have happened. Understandably, Frances did not want to go out, or speak to the press, and even checked the locks on the doors several times a day.

She had been incarcerated for only four days but it had seemed like a lifetime. The effect of poor diet, little water and damp conditions had left her with many sores and blemishes, but she cared little about that, knowing that these would heal. She hoped that her mind would mend as quickly.

The police explained that the man, or Gollum, as she called him, was Roland Whitehorn. He was born with a birth defect that made him look old and gave him odd bulbous, protruding eyes. His limbs were misshapen and he hobbled rather than walked. Physically abused by a father who had little time for a son so badly disabled, he also had to suffer the misfortune in a children's home to be mercilessly and endlessly goaded about his appearance and state of mind. As if this were not enough, he was also abused by a female member of staff who later went to prison for her misdeeds to him and other children. She subjected him to all kinds of sexual abuse.

Because of all this he never really developed mentally and suffered psychotic episodes that got blacker and blacker. He was prone to fits of anger and for his own and the safety of others he was sectioned under the Mental Health Act and placed in a secure hospital. Shortly afterwards, a slack nurse allowed him more freedom than he should and Roland ran away into the country never to be found again.

Three women's bodies and the carcass of poor Toby were found in shallow graves some way beyond the half sunken wartime bunker. Roland probably incarcerated and taunted them the way he had been; in his poor life, this had been the norm. Frances recalled the look of power in his face when he shooed her predecessor to the woods with a wave of his hand, knowing well that he would pursue her and his irrational fear at the sight of her breasts.

Now it was all over she pitied the poor man. A real deep pity for the life that he had been forced to lead when what he really needed was care and attention. It contrasted with her privileged, comfortable existence, free of pain and challenge. She didn't hate him any longer.

Standing up quietly, she left Phillip snoring in the armchair and walked around her lovely house, touching things occasionally as if she really didn't believe that she was home and safe. But how safe is anyone? The fearsome things a person can face in life are endless, but that it was not so much the event, but one's reaction to it that was the greatest challenge. There are many questions asked in times of extreme stress or danger, probing integrity, demanding strength of character and courage, all of which are easier to answer from the luxury of a false premise.

Frances leaned against the doorframe to Phillip's study and put her hand to her head, rubbing her temple.

Had she really been willing to do anything to get out of the bunker – absolutely anything? She would live with the touch of Gollum's clammy hand on her body forever, but most of all, it was her reluctance to cry out a warning to the young woman that scarred her pride. Frances tried to rationalise her action, by reasoning that it was acceptable given the end result. Once she was out of the bunker she would have gone for help and saved the other woman; but this was futile. She knew, oh yes, she knew, that she would have quickly put as much ground between her and her captor as she could, leaving her rescuer to fend for herself until help came much later. It would take her a long time to remove this shadow from her mind.

Seeing a faded photograph on top of sundry items on her husband's bookshelf she instinctively reached for it and as she drew it closer recognised the scene. It was a stone archway, with a human skull in a small niche in the wall, eyes hollow, teeth in a permanent eerie smile.

Above it, chiselled into the arch, were the words: *"Know Thyself."*

# Wrong Number

Helen tossed and turned in her bed, her arms and legs becoming entangled with the sheets and duvet. She had a terrible night's sleep, because her two-year old son Ben had cried several times and without a partner to take some of the strain it was exhausting. As she left deep slumber, she entered the cerebral waiting room before awakening, termed REM, where images are called up and mystifyingly fitted together in random visions. A dream had taken hold and she saw herself standing in a corridor, looking left and right.

Suddenly, the dreaming turned into a nightmare of smoke and flames, and her mind whirled as she heard her son, Ben, calling her and she felt a sense of peril. In this state, frighteningly, she couldn't move a muscle, no matter how she tried and this heightened her fear. Not being able to respond made her head buzz at her impotence. Eventually, the mist faded and her body gained coordination, and she awoke completely. Sitting up straight, heart pounding rapidly, she ran her hands through her sweaty hairline.

There was Ben, on the bottom of her duvet. Helen had broken all the rules and taken him into her bed, something she normally didn't do, but she had been beside herself with tiredness and relented.

Ben grinned at her and she noticed that he was holding her mobile phone to the side of his head, repeating, "Man, man…" He chuckled a little, as though he was talking to an old uncle. Normally he said something like 'hello', or at least it sounded like that, which made Helen laugh. But 'man' was a totally new word and really unusually clear.

Helen focussed unsteadily on Ben as he held the telephone out towards her.

"Man, man," he said again. She rubbed her eyes and reached for the phone. As she did so she heard a faint voice from the headset and she put it to her ear.

"I think you should give the phone to your mummy. Hello, little one, hello, do you hear me?" said the voice.

Helen cleared her throat of the night-time grunge and answered, "Hello, who is this please?"

"Ah, you must be the mummy."

"Yes, I am, and can I ask what you want please?"

"Well, you could, but since it was you, or at least your mobile phone, that called me and not the other way around that's a difficult question."

Helen paused and realised that Ben must have tried his luck at pushing buttons and dialled this man purely by chance.

"Oh, right then. Sorry, my fault," she said.

"Your fault?" said the man. "How can it be your fault?"

"For goodness sake," she said, irritably. "My son dialled, I was asleep, and it's my fault. Besides, you're a bloody man and it's a man-thing to want to apportion blame, so it's my fault. Can we leave it at that?"

The silence that followed seemed to last ages and for some strange reason that she couldn't fathom, she was unable to cut the call off. The man spoke again, this time a little more softly.

"Sorry, I was just being irritatingly logical. Please forgive me."

After a pause he added, "I get the feeling from what you just said that you've been through a tough time? Listen, I just picked up the phone and there was this lovely little voice calling me 'man'. It's nobody's fault, really. And for the record I've never quite fitted the model of manhood you just described. I suspect you are a single mum, and for that I give you all my admiration."

Helen gripped the sheets tightly, knotting them in her hands. She was so wound up and on edge, that someone talking nicely to her put a lump in her throat.

That was the way it had been for months now, ever since Gordon had dumped her. First it was her husband, Edward, who had walked out when Ben was barely four months old. Edward had a feckless, insouciant attitude to life that prevented him from earning a decent living. He found it easy to work at a rate lower than was sustainable on the basis that all he needed was a football season ticket and enough for a beer or two. It did not occur to him to value and provide for his family. This built into an unbearable stress, and inevitably

165

they rowed, but of course, when he left he told everyone that Helen was a nagging and demanding wife. So, the fingers pointed at her.

And then there was the omnipresent family friend, Gordon, who had been on hand to comfort her and was always there for her when she needed those man-jobs doing. Nothing had been too much trouble. Then he came onto her in a persuasive way. For a year he had insisted that his relationship with his wife had long since withered and that they were planning to separate when it was convenient. He said he was besotted with her and his attentiveness came at a time when she was vulnerable and needed it most – it made her feel good and she was easily snared.

Helen really liked him and thought the feeling was mutual. But time went on there was no sign of commitment. When she finally confronted him about leaving his wife he began to go cold on her, his calls dried up and eventually he left a message saying that he and his wife were 'making a go' of things and that he wouldn't be seeing her any more. He was sorry, blah, blah, blah.

In more clear-headed moments, she regretted not charging for the sex. His appetite had been insatiable and at least she would have earned money to pay the rent. But even this black humour didn't raise her spirits. There was little amusement these days and she seemed to be navigating through a red mist most of the time, devoid of love and without a way out of her world of little money and no companionship. It was Ben who had kept her sane - he plumbed into her affections, soaking up the love that was left.

Helen took a deep breath and accepted that the world, let alone the mystery male on the telephone, did not deserve her ire, and sat back against the bed headboard, at the same time helping Ben down onto the floor.

She cleared her throat.

"Look, I owe you an apology. That was crass of me. Yes, I've just been through a bit of a bad time lately and, well, it comes out some times. I'm sure you are a regular, nice guy. Sorry and all that, okay?"

"Jeez, now I feel bad young lady, this could go on forever, don't you know?"

Helen smiled at the thought of soppy reciprocal apologies and laughed out loud.

"Ah, now that's better," he said, "let's capitalise on that some time? But for now let me wish you well, oh and Ben of course."

"Yes, maybe, I mean, oh well, goodbye and all that. Thank you for chatting to my son," she said.

Before she could even ask his name the line went dead.

By now she was wide awake and decided to take a shower. Kissing Ben gently on his forehead, she slipped off the bed and out of her T-shirt top that doubled as a nightdress. As she did so, she saw Ben looking straight at her nakedness. It was just as though he was her ex, Edward, he too enjoyed sitting on the bed watching her undress and shower, or at her dressing table combing her long dark brown hair. So did Gordon. But for all their sensuality, and they both had much to commend them in that department, neither could connect with her needs as a woman, a person and not just a sex object. The need for respect, dignity, love and above all the understanding and sharing of decisions that affected her and Ben was all she wanted. It was not much to ask. She reached down for Ben's teddy bear and threw it to him and not waiting to see if he caught it, went to the shower room.

It was lunch-time and Helen was feeling a bit more cheerful and decided to take Ben to the local park. After collecting her benefits she had some cash in her pocket and decided to buy some ice cream and a coffee.

She found a space on a bench near the swings and slides, leaned back and let the rays of sunshine warm her face for a few moments. All of a sudden the red behind her eyes darkened and she realised that someone was standing in front of her.

She looked up and gasped. It was Alexis, Gordon's wife.

"Taking the sun?" she said with a hint of acid.

Helen felt her chest tighten. They had spent a lot of time together as a foursome, she and Edward, Alexis and Gordon. At one time they were inseparable. Now her stomach knotted at the mention of Alexis's name; it reminded her of the shameless way she had been seduced into adultery with Gordon.

She tried to speak but only stuttered.

"Yes, I, er..."

Alexis cut in.

"Don't feel awkward. I knew it was going on you know? Frankly, he was wearing me out and your split with Edward emboldened him to chase your tail."

She took out a packet of cigarettes and offered one to Helen.

"Cigarette? Oh, no, of course you don't. Fornication, yes, cigarettes, no. Heigh ho, each to her own eh?"

She lit the cigarette and let out a long stream of smoke. Helen wished she was somewhere else and reached for Ben's hand. He came to her easily.

"Look, I saw you and just wanted to let you know that, with me at least, there are no hard feelings. Women alone are either victims or hunters and frankly, even though I've known you for years I'm damned if I know which category you fit into. As for Gordon, I have him under tight wraps now. He's had his fling. Perhaps now he'll take up sailing, golf or an allotment, or something like that? But one more false move from him below the navel and above the knees and I'll take him for everything he's got. I'll rip his heart out – through his wallet of course!"

Alexis did not wait for an answer and walked away, without a backward glance. Helen cursed softly. Why couldn't she be like that? Why couldn't she demand compensation, repayment or anything else for that matter? As the tenseness began to recede, she felt Ben's arms around her shoulders. Of all the things that were most precious to her, her little boy was top of the list. She laughed – what bloody list? There was nothing of any value on any virtual list, or that wasn't on repayment or borrowed. So that was it then, Ben was the centre of her world. He was all she had and at the moment, all she wanted.

The sun's rays were diffused a little by low cloud, but it was nevertheless still very balmy and she tried hard to relax and de-stress after her confrontation with Alexis, with Ben wrapped in her arms. He fidgeted several times, but she thought nothing of it. About twenty minutes later, as she dozed, she heard Ben talking. It wasn't really talking of course, but it had the cadence of speech and always amused her. It was that special language developed by toddlers who desperately want to communicate, but haven't quite formed the vocabulary. He chuckled again.

Her eyes opened suddenly when he said the word, "Man, man…"

Helen sat up and brought Ben on to her knee. In his hand, close to his ear, he held her mobile phone he had taken from her handbag.

"Ben, you naughty boy, give it to mummy," she said, and he dutifully handed it to her. As he did so she heard a voice in the background.

She put the mobile phone to her ear.

"Hello?"

A voice replied, "Well hi, guess who?"

"Oh dear, I'm so sorry, I really am. Ben must have hit the redial key, I was asleep, you see and..."

"Asleep again? My goodness. How are you?"

Helen thought this intrusive but could only resort to sarcasm.

"Well, since you ask and seem to be taking an interest, courtesy of my little darling Ben, quite shitty actually. My ex-husband hasn't contacted his son or me for over a year and my ex-lover's wife just confronted me here in Priory Park and made me feel like a whore. But, tra-la-la, at least I picked up my benefits and can afford a double helping of chips tonight, so there is some light in my life."

Her voice began to quiver.

"And Ben..." said the man.

Helen thought for a few seconds and responded slowly.

"Yes," she said and stroked Ben's head. "And Ben, he's my light."

'Man' lightened the mood saying, "And what's more, he's a dab hand with the telephone you know. A bright young boy indeed. Perhaps he was trying to call his broker?"

Then there was silence and she got the weird feeling that he wanted to say something else and wasn't just making small talk. He duly obliged.

"Look, you deserve better than chips. Why not come to the community centre right now. It's a family affair, mums, dads and kids all having pizza and stuff like that."

Helen laughed and relaxed.

"Lovely man, I don't even know your name let alone which community centre, in which town, or in which part of the country you mean," she allowed herself a smile at his assumption that he knew where she was.

169

There was a silence as Helen hoped he would be put off. She had no enthusiasm at all to be with real families, that is, mums and dads together with their children, everyone happy and bouncy, their happiness the opposite to her world. It didn't really appeal to her and she tried to head off his reply.

"I'm not really sure that..."

The man cut her short, "But you must, you really must."

His voice had a strange urgency about it.

Helen was taken aback at the suddenness of his response. His manner was not the same as his earlier call.

She suddenly felt that she was letting him down.

"Listen, I know that you are just trying to be kind and I have shared too much with a stranger already, but I really don't want to go to a community centre that I don't know."

The man breathed out so hard she almost felt his breath down the phone. Then he said, more calmly, "I'm sorry. That was silly of me. I just wanted to help and that was really very clumsy. Let me just say, well, it would be to your advantage to go to the Aldridge Community Centre, that's the name, it's just down the road a bit, off Cavendish Road. It's quite near Priory Park as it happens. Go for a short while, just to please me. Now, how's that for a big ask?"

Helen didn't know whether to get annoyed or see the funny side of the conversation, especially the appeal to please someone she didn't even know.

"Are you sure my son called you and not the other way around?"

"Heavens above, yes, what do you think?"

Before she could answer he added, "Besides, did you hear the phone ring, no, I doubt it. So no more doubting me, eh? Okay, that's one point to me and I make it my game call, so go to the Aldridge Community Centre, just for a while. Go on now, please, for me?"

His plea actually touched her. Here was a man trying to get her to do something, but instead of coercion or aggressiveness he was being amusing and persuasive. She could say, yes, or no, but he really wanted her to say, yes, and was working hard on her, taking nothing for granted, but being nice about it. For some odd reason that actually felt good.

"Okay then, mister persuasive, I've got nothing else to do. Who shall I ask for?"

"Ask for Grant," he said.

"Grant it is then. Strange. You don't sound like a Grant to me?"

"Just ask for Grant. You promise me that you won't go back to the flats without visiting the community centre first?"

"Yes, yes, I will do just that. I look forward to meeting you," but as she said that, the line went dead.

It took Helen only fifteen minutes to walk from the park to the Aldridge Community Centre, which was located between two large blocks of flats just like her own. There was clearly a fun day going on and she joined the throng of people milling around stalls and café style seating. What to do next? Walking past a large glass window she caught sight of herself. Her loose fitting blue print dress was a little dated but it looked good, however her hair looked a mess and needed combing. She headed for the ladies room. When she was finishing her make up she turned to an older lady who was on her way out.

"Excuse me, I'm her to meet someone called Grant, do you know him?"

"Why yes, dear, I know him very well. I can take you to him if you like. He is a lovely man," she replied with a kind of effusive manner that surprised Helen.

Together they walked through the crowded community centre, avoiding parents who were too busy talking to each other and small children who were hell bent on colliding with everything that crossed their path. Every five yards or so the woman looked over her shoulder with a kind of concern that seemed to indicate that she was afraid Helen would get lost.

A few minutes later they stood in front of a large Punch and Judy box.

"Grant, there's a lady here to see you. Where are you?" said the woman, who was about to peek under the curtain when all of a sudden the puppet Judy looked over the top of the stage and said loudly, "Dewdy dewdy dew, what shall I do?"

The woman jumped and Ben convulsed with laughter. It made Helen laugh spontaneously. She hadn't done that for a long time.

Then for the next ten minutes, Punch appeared and played to Judy and she found herself sitting cross-legged with Ben and another little girl, with golden hair and bright blue eyes, who joined them.

The show ended and they applauded loudly. There was no one else around.

Out from behind the curtain came a blonde haired man, not unlike Robert Redford in looks, but perhaps a little less self-assured.

"Hello audience. How was that? Not too popular with the other three hundred people though?" he said, waving his right arm in the direction of the burger bar.

Helen smiled. "Well it was with us. Wasn't that good, Ben?"

Ben smiled and nodded, pointing to the Punch puppet, which he was duly given to play with.

"That was kind of you," said Helen. "Now don't break it, Ben, there's a good boy. My name's, Helen Barclay, by the way. Well now. Thanks for encouraging me to come along, Grant."

"Er, I'm sorry, did I miss something?" he said.

Helen was puzzled.

"The mobile phone conversations, remember? You encouraged me to come to the community centre. You said to ask for Grant."

"Sorry, Helen. I really don't recall doing that. I do have the odd tipple from time to time, but today is my non-alcoholic day."

He pulled a sane but funny face and despite the concern building inside her, she felt strangely relaxed with this man and didn't want to probe further. The voice said to ask for Grant, not that he was Grant. Besides, now she was talking to this chap it was clear that both voices were different. What the hell was going on? Was all that a bad dream – two bad dreams in one day?

Helen decided to ignore the confusion for the moment. Grant was a good-looking guy and had a nice personality, so she resolved to stay. She was glad she did. The rest of the afternoon was sublime; relaxed and happy she watch Ben play with Grant's daughter Lucy, the little girl who had joined them earlier. Helen came out of herself, as she hadn't done for such a long time. Grant told her that he was without a partner, and then, when he was more comfortable added that his wife had died of breast cancer, leaving him with a daughter to bring up alone. It wasn't until they finally stopped talking about

172

their lives, what had happened to them, their hopes and fears for the future, and strained the last cup from the community centre coffee machine, that they realised they were the last two people left in the centre. The cleaners were filling black plastic sacks with the day's rubbish. The security man was stomping around irritably, clearly wanting them to leave. It was now eight o'clock.

Grant looked up.

"Crikey, it's nearly my shift time. Helen, I have never been so reluctant to go and earn money, but I am afraid I have to. I need to get Lucy to a child-minder. Can I walk you home?"

Helen thought that was such a cute line, no one had asked to walk her home for such a long time.

"No, not at all, it's not far, thank you. Yes, it has been fun." Then she added without thinking, "I'm so glad I came to the centre."

They both fidgeted about, gathering bags and then said goodbye, but not before exchanging telephone numbers. Perhaps they could meet – after all, the children were getting on so well – why not?

Then they parted, awkwardly, as people who are attracted to each other for the first time do - unable to kiss, too formal to shake hands and yet unfulfilled with the giving of a gentle half wave and a "...bye for now..."

Helen took the long route home around the edge of the park, walking slowly and thinking about the pleasant time she and Ben had just had. It was still quite light and she was able to walk and think to herself. The flat held too many memories and she wanted to celebrate this beautiful encounter without being reminded that men are not always what they seem to be. She walked down the small road to the block of flats and hardly heard the yells of children rushing towards it. She was lost in her thoughts.

As she approached where she lived she realised why there was considerable excitement all around her. Then looked up and saw why. The whole apartment block, from the middle upwards was a sheet of flame and in an instant she realised that all her possessions had gone up in smoke. Two fire engines were positioned with ladders extended to enable water to be sprayed on the flames at different levels.

Without thinking and mesmerised, she walked closer to the block.

"Oh no, Ben, look, our home is on fire."

She was so shocked that she hardly felt his hand slip from hers and he ran headlong across the path and towards the smoke filled doorway, shouting "Pooky, Pooky, Pooky," the name of his teddy bear.

Helen screamed frantically with fear, but the smoke made her cough and her voice failed. Her feet were anchored to the ground in shock. She put her hands to her head and tears streamed down her face mixing with smoke as she tried to follow Ben. Several pairs of hands restrained her and she struggled as only a mother can in such circumstances, her mind in turmoil.

As she watched Ben running towards the doorway, transfixed with terror, a fireman stepped out of the smoke and scooped up the boy. It was a tall blonde man, dressed in protective gear and carrying his large yellow helmet. He looked up, recognised Helen immediately and without breaking step strode towards her.

It was Grant.

"My God Helen, do you live here? What a good job we talked for so long otherwise you might have been part of all this carnage. It was a gas leak and explosion. Some people didn't make it. But Ben is okay, look, just a bit of smoke in his lungs."

Helen cried and hugged Ben as though she would never ever let go of him again. He coughed a bit but was otherwise quite safe and unharmed. She held onto him tightly. Thanks to sympathetic neighbours, she was taken back to the community centre, tea and blankets were provided and time went past in a haze of comforting words. And then it was all over. The fire engines stopped their work, one was designated to remain on station and the other departed for other emergency cover.

One lone fire fighter remained in the area, it was Grant. He walked into the centre and towards Helen who looked up at him. She felt his hand gently touch her shoulder.

"Are you all right? That must have been such a terrible shock for you. Ben is fine. He's here with you now, happy as anything. Okay? But I must say it was a very close call. Five more minutes and he would've been up the stairs in search of Pooky."

All Helen could do was to nod. She wanted to thank him so much, but was in a state of shock.

"Helen, I know this is going to sound very pushy, but I don't mean it to be. I have a large house not three miles away. You have nowhere to live now and need to sort stuff out with social services and so on."

He paused, took a deep breath and nervously went on, "Why not come back with me. My Lucy will play with Ben and you can relax. I promise that this is just a platonic offer of help – separate bedrooms and all that."

Helen's eyes filled with tears and she looked up at him, nodding slowly in agreement, biting the left side of her lip with her eye-tooth as she did so, making the skin go white.

Then Grant's face softened.

"Oh damnation, I lied. Sorry, yes, I lied. You can stay Helen, of course you can, until you get sorted out, but I have to admit that I like you a lot. I liked you the minute I met you. We talked so well and frankly I just felt that I know you already – crazy, but there you go. So every bloody minute you are with me I will be trying to get to know you and Ben a bit more, and I will do my best to impress you to stay with me longer. It's your choice, of course. I just don't want to lie to you that's all. You deserve better than that."

Helen said nothing and allowed herself to be he helped up. Then she unselfconsciously put her arm around his waist. For some uncanny reason she felt perfectly safe with Grant.

As they walked down the corridor, they passed a large ornately framed photograph of a kindly looking middle-aged man that was mounted at the entrance to the centre. Grant explained that he had been cited for bravery and awarded the George Medal. Mister Geoffrey Aldridge, saved several people from a fire in a block of flats nearby, in the nineteen sixties, but sadly lost his wife and son in the conflagration. He died of heartbreak barely six months later, but was fondly remembered by the local people. That was why the building was called the Aldridge Community Centre.

Helen, Grant and Ben slowly went through the front doors to the car park, the adults bent towards each other and Ben lightly holding Helen's hand.

Barely two steps outside, Ben stopped suddenly, turned around and looked back at the picture and steadily pointed at it.

He said loudly, "Man, Mummy, Man!"